The Great
Fairy Tale Classics

TORMONT

ILLUSTRATIONS: Piero Cattaneo
Tony Wolf
Severino Baraldi

TEXT: Peter Holeinone

© DAMI EDITORE, ITALY

Published by:
TORMONT PUBLICATIONS INC.
338 St. Antoine St. East
Montreal, Canada
Tel.: (514) 954-1441   Fax: (514) 954-1443

ISBN 2-921171-29-5
Printed in Canada

CONTENTS

CINDERELLA	5
THE SNOW MAIDEN	14
SAYED'S ADVENTURES	16
THE EMPRESS JOWKA	26
THE BOOK OF SPELLS	34
THE GAME OF CHESS	38
BLUEBEARD	44
THE TIN SOLDIER	53
THE ELVES AND THE SHOEMAKER	62
THE TAIL OF THE BEAR	64
THE SHREWD FARMER'S STORY	66
JACK AND THE BEANSTALK	70
THE EMPEROR'S NEW CLOTHES	79
SIX ABLE MEN	84
THE SEVEN CROWS	92
THE ADVENTURES OF ALADDIN	101
ALI BABA AND THE FORTY THIEVES	112
THE PARROT SHAH	124
THE WEEPING PRINCESS	134
SASHA, MANSOR AND THE STORKS	140
PUSS IN BOOTS	149
TIL ULENSPIGHEL	158
THE PEASANT, THE SNAKE AND THE FOX	164
THE WITCH IN THE TOWER	170
THE SEVEN OLD SAMURAI	172
THE UNLUCKY WARRIOR	176
THE RED DRAGON	180
DOPEY DENNIS	182
THE SLEEPING PRINCESS	190
SINBAD THE SAILOR	197
PRINCE OMAR AND PRINCESS SHEHERAZADE	224
THE FLYING TRUNK	234
THE LITTLE PEAR GIRL	236
THE SNOW QUEEN	240

Once upon a time . . .

. . . there lived an unhappy young girl. Unhappy she was, for her mother was dead, her father had married another woman, a widow with two daughters, and her stepmother didn't like her one little bit.

CINDERELLA

All the nice things, kind thoughts and loving touches were for her own daughters. And not just the kind thoughts and love, but also dresses, shoes, shawls, delicious food, comfy beds, as well as every home comfort. All this was laid on for her daughters. But, for the poor unhappy girl, there was nothing at all. No dresses, only her stepsisters' hand-me-downs. No lovely dishes, nothing but scraps. No nice rests and comfort. For *she* had to work hard all day, and only when evening came was she allowed to sit for a while by the fire, near the cinders. That is how she got her nickname, for everybody called her Cinderella. Cinderella used to spend long hours all alone talking to the cat. The cat said,

"Miaow", which really meant, "Cheer up! You have something neither of your stepsisters have and that is beauty."

It was quite true. Cinderella, even dressed in rags with a dusty grey face from the cinders, was a lovely girl. While her stepsisters, no matter how splendid and elegant their clothes, were still clumsy, lumpy and ugly and always would be.

One day, beautiful new dresses arrived at the house. A ball was to be held at Court and the stepsisters were getting ready to go to it. Cinderella didn't even dare ask, "What about me?" for she knew very well what the answer to that would be

"You? My dear girl, you're staying at home to wash the dishes, scrub the floors and turn down the beds for your stepsisters. They will come home tired and very sleepy." Cinderella sighed at the cat,

"Oh dear, I'm so unhappy!" and the cat murmured "Miaow".

Suddenly something amazing happened. In the kitchen, where Cinderella was sitting all by herself, there was a burst of light and a fairy appeared.

"Don't be alarmed, Cinderella," said the fairy. "The wind blew me your sighs. I know you would love to go to the ball. And so you shall!"

"How can I, dressed in rags?" Cinderella replied. "The servants will turn me away!" The fairy smiled. With a flick of her magic wand. . . . Cinderella found herself wearing the most beautiful dress, the loveliest ever seen in the realm.

"Now that we have settled the matter of the dress," said the fairy, "we'll need to get you a coach. A real lady would never go to a ball on foot!"

"Quick! Get me a pumpkin!" she ordered.

"Oh of course," said Cinderella, rushing away. Then the fairy turned to the cat.

"You, bring me seven mice!"

"Seven mice!" said the cat. "I didn't know fairies ate mice too!"

"They're not for eating, silly! Do as you are told! . . . and, remember they must be alive!"

Cinderella soon returned with a fine pumpkin and the cat with seven mice he had caught in the cellar.

"Good!" exclaimed the fairy. With a flick of her magic wand . . . wonder of wonders! The pumpkin turned into a sparkling coach and the mice became six white horses, while the seventh mouse turned into a coachman, in a smart uniform and carrying a whip. Cinderella could hardly believe her eyes.

"I shall present you at Court. You will soon see that the Prince, in whose honour the ball is being held, will be enchanted by your loveliness. But remember! You must leave the ball at midnight and come home. For that is when the spell ends. Your coach will turn back into a pumpkin, the horses will become mice again and the coachman too will turn back into a mouse . . . and you will be dressed again in rags and wearing clogs instead of these dainty little slippers! Do you understand?" Cinderella smiled and said,

"Yes, I understand!"

When Cinderella entered the ballroom at the palace, a hush fell. Everyone stopped in mid-sentence to admire her elegance, her beauty and grace.

"Who can that be?" people asked each other. The two stepsisters also wondered who the newcomer was, for never in a month of Sundays, would they ever have guessed that the beautiful girl was really poor Cinderella who talked to the cat!

When the prince set eyes on Cinderella, he was struck by her beauty. Walking over to her, he bowed deeply and asked her to dance. And to the great disappointment of all the young ladies, he danced with Cinderella all evening.

"Who are you, fair maiden?" the Prince kept asking her. But Cinderella only replied:

"What does it matter who I am! You will never see me again anyway."

"Oh, but I shall, I'm quite certain!" he replied.

Cinderella had a wonderful time at the ball . . . But, all of a sudden, she heard the sound of a clock: the first stroke of midnight! She remembered what the fairy had said, and without a word of goodbye she slipped from the Prince's arms and ran down the steps. As she ran she lost one of her slippers, but not for a moment did she dream of stopping to pick it up! If the last stroke of midnight were to sound . . . oh . . . what a disaster that would be! Out she fled and vanished into the night.

The Prince, who was now madly in love with her, picked up her slipper and said to his ministers,

"Go and search everywhere for the girl whose foot this slipper fits. I will never be content until I find her!" So the ministers tried the slipper on the foot of all the girls . . . and on Cinderella's foot as well . . . Surprise! The slipper fitted perfectly.

"That awful untidy girl simply cannot have been at the ball," snapped the stepmother. "Tell the Prince he ought to marry one of my two daughters! Can't you see how ugly Cinderella is! Can't you see?"

Suddenly she broke off, for the fairy had appeared.

"That's enough!" she exclaimed, raising her magic wand. In a flash, Cinderella appeared in a splendid dress, shining with youth and beauty. Her stepmother and stepsisters gaped at her in amazement, and the ministers said,

"Come with us, fair maiden! The Prince awaits to present you with his engagement ring!" So Cinderella joyfully went with them, and lived happily ever after with her Prince. And as for the cat, he just said "Miaow"!

THE SNOW MAIDEN

Once upon a time there was a beautiful garden which became even more beautiful that day, after a heavy fall of snow covered the ground, the trees and bushes in a soft white mantle. A little boy and girl were playing happily in the garden, they were brother and sister.

They chased each other, threw snowballs and played hide and seek under the fir trees. Then the little girl said,

"Let's make a snow doll."

They began to make the doll and decided it would be a girl.

"So there will be three of us and we'll have more fun!" said the little girl. So they carefully built a doll made of snow, with a pretty oval face, long hair, large eyes and a delicate little mouth. It looked just like a real little girl.

"Let's give her a kiss and maybe her lips will turn red like ours," said the sister. So they kissed the doll . . . and lo and behold, its lips turned red!

And the snow doll's cheeks turned pink. When a sudden gust of wind blew from the north, the doll came to life. It moved, smiled at the two children and started to play with them.

Some time later, the children's father returned from town. When he saw the girl in white playing with his own children, he said to himself,

"It must be one of the neighbour's daughters." Then he said to the little snow doll, "Come into the house and get warm." But the snow maiden made a frightened sign as though to say "No!" The man, however led her into the house, saying,

"Oh, you're so cold! The fire will soon warm you up!" But the snow maiden sighed sadly, though she didn't have the courage to speak. In she went and stood by the window, looking out at the white garden. Then she began to weep – and slowly and gently, she began to melt . . . until nothing was left of her except a trace of white snow on the floor. . . .

SAYED'S ADVENTURES

Once upon a time, in the mysterious East, lived a man called Benezar who married a woman named Zemira. They were in love with each other and agreed on all things, except one. Zemira believed in magic, omens, premonitions and fairies. Benezar only believed in what he could see before his eyes. However, that did not mar their happiness at all, and this reached its height, when, one day, in the midst of a thunderstorm, Zemira gave birth to a handsome baby boy. When Benezar, who had anxiously awaited the arrival, was allowed to see the baby, he noticed a tiny whistle hanging from a thin silver thread round its neck.

"What's this?" he asked.

"It's a gift a fairy made to our son," replied Zemira. "It's a magic gift. Take it," she went on, removing the whistle from the child's neck, "give it to our son when he is twenty."

"All right. But listen, what are we to call the child?" asked Benezar.

"Sayed," replied Zemira.

The years went by and Sayed grew healthy, strong and brave. He was eighteen years old when he decided to go on a pilgrimage to the holy city of Mecca. He told his father of his decision.

"Yes, I'm pleased you're going," said his father. "In fact, Sayed, take this as a lucky charm," and he gave him the fairy's gift.

"What is it?" Sayed asked.

"It's a whistle. Your mother, alas now dead, thought highly of it. Carry it with you always."

"I will father," said the young man, putting the whistle round his neck.

Not long after, the travellers with a hundred camels, many merchants and a host of guards, set out on the journey. Young Sayed was splendidly equipped and armed with a sword, spear, bow and arrows.

It was a long, long way to the holy city of Mecca. They travelled over plains, mountains and deserts. It was on a long stretch of desert that they were attacked by a large band of robbers. They were caught unaware, some tried to flee, but Sayed shouted:

"Flee? Where do you think you can flee to in the desert? Come on. Let's die fighting!" and he hurled himself against the attackers. At the height of the fighting, Sayed was attacked by a young robber, richly dressed and riding a white horse. The young man bravely faced his attacker and killed him with his sword. A soldier nearby shouted out,

"What have you done? You've killed Almansor. This is the end, let's run!" Men ran in all directions. Now practically alone Sayed remembered the whistle round his neck. If it really was magic, it might be able to help him . . . he put it to his lips and blew hard . . . But nothing happened. Not so much as a whisper of sound.

In the meantime, the others had fled. Sayed was taken prisoner, bound and led before Sheik Selim, a very powerful man, the leader of several of the desert tribes and, unfortunately, the father of Almansor, the very man Sayed had killed. Selim, however, was not an unjust man. When he discovered that Sayed had taken Almansor's life in a fair fight, he refused to allow a hair of his head to be harmed. Indeed, he

set him free and entrusted the young man to some travellers

about to leave for far off Mecca, the holy city.

Sayed thus found himself once more on his travels. However, one night, friends of the dead Almansor captured him.

"Your master told you not to kill me," cried the young man.

"We're not going to kill you. All we're going to do is tie you up and leave you here in the desert. Thirst and the sun, or the vultures or the jackals will do the rest. They, not us, will kill you!" And laughing cruelly, they rode away. Two whole days went by. Sayed was on the point of death, baked by the sun and with no water, when close by passed some travellers belonging to Kalum the merchant. They came to his aid and saved his life.

As he came back to his senses with the first sips of water, Sayed spoke:

"May Allah reward you, Sir, for saving my life. What is your name?"

"My name is Kalum," said the man, "but it won't be Allah who will reward me. You are going to do that yourself. If I hadn't come along, you would have been dead by now. And you are going to work for me until you have repaid that debt. What is your name?"

"Sayed," he answered.

"Well, Sayed, get up and come with me." The young man went along with Kalum and on the way discovered that he was a rich merchant from Baghdad, so that was the city in which he went to live. At that time, Baghdad was ruled by the famous Caliph, Harun-el-Rascid, wise, valiant and loved by all. Kalum owned a big bazaar in the city and it was there that Sayed was put to work doing all the humble jobs.

One day, a veiled woman came to the bazaar. Sayed was amazed when she said to him,

"You're Sayed, aren't you?"

"Yes," he replied in astonishment. "How did you know that?"

"Tell me, have you still got the whistle round your neck?"

"Of course!" exclaimed the young man. "You must be the fairy who gave it to my mother. But what is this whistle *for*? I've tried blowing it, but . . ." The woman interrupted him.

"It will be of no use to you until you are twenty. Then it will save your life. Now tell me, what can I do for you?"

"Help me to get home," Sayed replied. "I need lots of money for that, which I don't have."

"But you're brave and strong. You can earn it," said the woman, and she explained that, every week, tournaments were held in the city, and Harun-el-Rascid, the Caliph, always watched them. The winners received rich prizes. The veiled woman had weapons, armour and horses and she lent these to Sayed. He took part in the tournaments and always beat the others, winning lots of prizes, as well as the Caliph's admiration. Sayed, however, never revealed his name, but just mentioned that he was a horseman from distant Cairo.

Now it so happens that the Caliph, Harun-el-Rascid, liked to wander through the city at night, disguised as a beggar or merchant, to hear what folk had to say about him. Not to spy on them, but to try and put right any mistakes he might have made. Sometimes, he was accompanied by his chief minister. Well, one night, as Sayed was going home to Kalum's bazaar, he heard shouts and the sounds of struggle. Four men had attacked two others in a dark corner. The brave young man immediately came to the rescue by killing two of the attackers and chasing the others away. When it was all over, the two victims thanked Sayed and asked him,

"Brave youth, what's your name?"

"My name is Sayed," came the reply.

"I'm Kalum the merchant's shop assistant."

"Hmm," said one of the two men, "you seem to be more of a gentleman than a shop assistant. However, take this ring as a reward for what you did for me." Then the other man spoke,

"And this bag of coins. You've saved my life and you deserve it. Goodbye!" And away they went.

Sayed stood there with the ring and bag in his hand. With these he could now find a ship and go home.

Next day, he said to Kalum,

"I'm leaving. I shan't be working for you any longer."

"And where are you going to?" asked Kalum.

"Home!" answered Sayed.

"Home? But it's a costly journey, and with the wages I pay you . . ." Sayed smiled,

"Your pay certainly wouldn't take me far, but . . ." and he held out the bag, "but this money will. Farewell!" However, wicked Kalum was not to be defeated. He told the police Sayed had stolen a bag of gold. The young man was immediately arrested. The chief of police asked him,

"Who gave you this money?"

"A man I'd never seen before," was the honest reply. Sayed was judged a thief and sentenced to deportation to Thirsty Island, the home of the worst kind of criminals. On the ship the young man thought to himself, "Well, I left home two years ago, proud, rich and happy. Here I am today, twenty years old, in the midst of these convicts, condemned to live and die an innocent man in prison!"

During the night there was a terrible storm. Driven by the wind, the ship was flung about by the waves until it crashed onto some hidden rocks.

Only one man survived the disaster. It was Sayed. At the mercy of the waters, he groped for something to hold on to, but nothing came within his grasp, until he suddenly felt his fingers touch the whistle the fairy had given him. Desperately, he blew it . . . and a dolphin surfaced beside him, shaking its head as though to tell him to get onto its back. Sayed clambered up and there found safety. He remembered the fairy had told him that when he was twenty years old, the whistle would save his life! The dolphin carried the young man within sight of land.

"Thanks, friend!" called out Sayed as he slid down from the creature and swam ashore. What a surprise awaited him! There was a military camp, soldiers and war machines. Sayed was taken prisoner and brought before none other than Harun-el-Rascid himself. The soldiers who had seized him said,

"Sire, this man must be one of the convicts that survived the shipwreck."

"Is that so?" Harun-el-Rascid demanded gravely.

"Yes," replied Sayed, "I did survive the shipwreck. But I'm not a convict." And he explained how he had been reported to the police because of the bag of gold. "It was given to me," he went on, "by one of two men I saved one night from being attacked by four robbers." Harun-el-Rascid looked at the man sitting beside him and then said,

"Did the two men give you anything else?"

"Yes, they did, this ring," Sayed replied, showing the Caliph the ring which he kept round his neck with the whistle. Harun rose to his feet and exclaimed:

"Young man, the two men you helped were my chief minister and myself! Go free, but first tell me your name."

"Sayed, Sire."

"Sayed?" echoed the chief minister. "There's a man here in the camp called Benezar, who is searching for his son Sayed." "It's my father!" cried the young man. And it was his father. They hugged each other in delight.

Since justice must be done in the world, evil Kalum was arrested and imprisoned as he deserved to be . . . .

THE EMPRESS JOWKA

Once upon a time . . . an Empress lived in Japan. She was young, beautiful, kindly, and wise, and her name was Jowka. She dreamt of living in peace, thinking of the welfare of her people, but in the northern mountains, a rebellion broke out led by Prince Kokai. He sent a message to the Empress,

"Jowka, either you must marry me and share the throne, or I will put your kingdom to the flame and sword!" Jowka, who knew that empresses never flinch at threats, replied,

"Kokai, we shall fight!", and sent an army against the rebels. The army was strong and well led and it defeated the rebels in more than one battle. But, just before the most important battle of all, something terrible and magical happened.

Kokai pleaded with one of the evil gods and it started to rain. The rivers grew swollen with water and broke their banks. There were appalling floods which took the Imperial army by surprise and swept it away. Every man, from the general to the humblest soldier, was drowned. And Kokai the rebel came down from the mountains and approached the capital of the Empire. Jowka sent other armies against him, but each one met the same fate: swept away in the swirling waters that obeyed Kokai's orders. The whole of Japan was terror-stricken. Was power to be seized by a merciless rebel magician?

Jowka was lost in thought over this when, one night, she heard a rustle in the room where she was saying her prayers. Lifting her eyes, she saw, standing in front of her, a man wearing a long tunic and holding a stick. He had long white hair and a flowing beard, as soft as silk. The Empress jumped in surprise, but the old man said:

"Have no fear, Jowka, I'm a friend. I'm the God of Fire. I heard your prayers, I know how much you are suffering, and I'm here to help. Don't worry! I shall join your armies and Kokai's magic will do nothing against me."

"Tell me, God of Fire, what must I do?" the Empress murmured.

"You must gather a new army to send against the rebel. I will march at the side of your general." And so the Empress ordered the greatest and biggest army ever seen in Japan to be mustered, and a huge number of men, horses and chariots set out.

Everyone, including the Imperial and the rebel soldiers, knew that the battle about to be fought would be final. The two opposing armies slowly drew closer on a vast plain, and the general leading the imperial troops murmured:

"It is unwise to march here. Kokai could easily flood this area!" The God of Fire, marching at the general's side in the guise of a bold young officer said:

"Have no fear, I'm far stronger than water." There were a few skirmishes, then Kokai, high on the mountain where he had made his camp, raised his arms invoking the help of the elements. The earth shook, there was a fierce gust of wind and an immense rush of water swept down the mountainside onto the plain. The Imperial soldiers screamed with terror, but the God of Fire simply said:

"Keep calm! That water will not even lap our feet." And indeed, the huge foaming waves that seemed to gallop towards the army, suddenly slowed down when they reached the God of Fire, drew back, split with a tremendous roar and were swallowed up by the earth.

"This is the end of Kokai! March on!" ordered the general, and the entire army marched on towards the mountain and defeated the enemy. Kokai saw that the rebellion was now over, his power had gone and his fortune too had disappeared. But rather than surrender to the Empress Jowka, who would have forgiven him, he hurled himself, head first, against the mountain and died. But the blow was so hard that the mountain, named Shu, cracked and from the crack gushed out fire, poisonous fumes and lava, that quickly invaded the plain below, burning and suffocating everything on it. A far worse danger now threatened the empire of the wise Jowka!

The Empress remained quite calm. Then she received another terrible piece of news. The crack in the mountain and the disaster that followed, had also cracked the pillars that held up the sky, damaging the pathway along which, every day, the Sun and the Moon travelled with their chariots, carrying the light.

In a short time, in fact, a dreadful dark shadow fell over all the world. People were afraid of the darkness, they wept and despaired. So wise Jowka ordered huge bonfires to be kept alight, so that the flames would give them comfort, courage and new hope. And she sent word to all her subjects that they should collect blue, white, black, orange and red stones and bring them to the palace. When that was done, the Empress ground down the stones, and made a kind of paste, something like liquid porcelain, transparent and shiny.

She put it in a pot, then with a magic spell summoned a cloud, climbed on top of it and made it carry her to the exact spot where the heavenly pillar was cracked. There, she repaired the damage using the strange coloured paste. As she went back to earth, she said to herself, "There! The pillar is mended. The chariots of the Sun and the Moon can take to the road again and the light will return." Alas! Things didn't quite happen that way! Days went by and the light had still not come back. The Sun and the Moon were nowhere to be seen. And the people, who had had such high hopes, again began to weep and wail. Everyone began to say, "Oh dear! We shall live the rest of our lives in the dark! We will go blind, we will die of the cold! Nothing will grow in the fields, and if we survive the dark and the cold, we will die of hunger!"

Once again, the Empress kept calm and was unworried. She called together all the wise men of the realm and asked them to find out what had happened. Long discussions took place, then a very learned philosopher went before Jowka and told her,

"Your most gracious Highness, I know exactly what has happened! When the pillar of heaven cracked, the Sun and the Moon shut themselves away in their palaces in alarm. And they have never come out again. How can they possibly know the pillar has been repaired?"

"Yes! Yes! That is so!" chorussed the other wise men. The Empress then said, "There is only one way to tell them. Send a messenger!"

"A messenger?" they asked. Jowka went on.

"Yes. Or rather, two! One to gallop to the Sun and the other to the Moon. We can't be discourteous, and if we were to warn one before the other, then the second one might take offence." All over the empire, a search was made for two horsemen brave enough to face such a long journey, and two horses strong enough to gallop into the heart of Day and Night. It wasn't easy to find suitable men but in the end, two young men came to Jowka, and she told them what had to be done . . .

The messengers set off. It was a long and fearful journey, from cloud to cloud, from heaven to heaven, through winds and storms, brushing past comets and shooting stars. But they delivered the Empress's message to the Sun and the Moon. The pillar had been repaired, their chariots could return to the heavenly pathways. The Sun and the Moon thanked the messengers.

The next day, the shadows disappeared from the daylight world, and light flooded back again, as before. The two messengers knelt before the Empress on their return, but Jowka made them rise to their feet, saying:

"No! Men like you shall always remain on their feet before anyone on earth, for you have looked the Sun and the Moon in the face!"

33

THE BOOK OF SPELLS

Once upon a time . . . in the middle of a forest round whose edges lay scattered some peasants cottages, an ogre used to live. He was big, cruel and heartless, but he liked his house to be tidy. So he said to himself,

"I'm always out hunting, fishing and causing trouble. I need somebody to look after the house, clean the floors, wash the plates and do the laundry every week . . ." Out he went and crouched down near one of the cottages, belonging to certain poor peasants.

When he saw their children come out, a boy and a girl, he stretched out his big hand, grabbed them and carried them away.

"You'll be my servants," he said, "and I will give you your food. But if you try to run away, you will be the next dish!" Terrified, the two children agreed, and they lived in the ogre's house for a long time. Then, they noticed that, every evening, the ogre pulled out a large book, which he would read carefully

. . . it was the Book of Spells! The two children, who were intelligent, read the book when the ogre was away, and they too learned the magic spells. At last, the boy said,

"Sister, I think I know enough now! Come on, let's run away!"

"Oh! Are you sure you know how to cast spells?" asked the girl anxiously.

"Of course!" said he. "Come on, before the ogre gets back!" So the pair ran out of the house and into the forest. Suddenly, the girl cried out,

"I can hear somebody running! The ogre's following us!" The ogre was determined to catch the pair and, without a doubt, with his long legs, he would soon catch up on them.

So the young lad cast the first of the spells. He turned himself into a pond and his sister into a minnow! A moment later, the ogre rushed up, saw what had taken place and growled:

"If only I had a line! I'll run and fetch one!" and off he went. The two children turned back into their normal selves and started to flee once more. But the ogre was soon on their heels and he was just about to lay hands on them, when the boy cast the second spell. He turned himself into a shrine and his sister into an angel painted on the wall. The ogre would have loved to kick the shrine to bits, but he didn't dare. He shouted,

"I'll burn you down instead!" and ran to fetch a bundle of wood.

In the meantime, however, the children were off again. They ran and ran, till they were exhausted and out of breath . . . And on the point of being snatched . . . the boy, working a third spell, turned himself and his sister into grains of corn, that mingled with thousands and thousands of other grains on the threshing floor . . . The ogre exclaimed:

"You think you can beat me with my own spells, but I'm far more cunning than you!" and he turned into a cockerel that hurriedly began to peck all the grains. What awful danger. But a second before being pecked, the boy turned into a fox, pounced on the cockerel and gobbled him up!

And now that the ogre was gone, the boy and his sister were able to go home again, safe and sound!

THE GAME OF CHESS

Once upon a time . . . in faraway Persia there was a King who had a beautiful wife and a handsome son called Gav. Life was all sunshine as far as he was concerned, but not for long.

One day, as he was going hunting, he fell from his horse and was killed. Women in Persia could not succeed to the throne and so the dead ruler's brother was proclaimed King. He was a prince called May. He fell in love with the widowed Queen and married her. She gave him a son whose name was Talend. Alas, some time later, the new King died and there only remained the Queen with the two sons, brothers of course, but with different fathers. The question was soon raised:–

"Which brother will become King of Persia?" "It will be Gav," was one reply, "because he is the elder." But others said, "It will be Talend, because he is the son of our last King." The Queen herself said nothing at all.

However, sooner or later, she would have to come to a decision, and she did not want to disappoint either Gav or Talend. As long as the two boys were small, it didn't matter, but when they started to grow up and began to ask when one or the other was going to be crowned King, the problems began. The Queen couldn't make up her mind. When her ministers asked her to make a choice, she would reply,

"Yes, I will do it tomorrow . . ." and so the years went by.

Gav and Talend became young men, and rivals. As children they were always together, as youths, they saw little of each other, indeed, they kept out of each other's way. Each had his own set of friends. In that way, two sides were formed, one supporting Talend, the other supporting Gav. The ministers were very worried, and now insisted that the Queen choose the King. But she couldn't bring herself to do this, for fear of disappointing one of her dearly loved sons.

Some years later, the kingdom drifted towards what is known as civil war, for the two princes did not see eye to eye, neither wanted to give up the throne, neither wanted to step down. Some of the provinces sided with Talend, others with Gav. Certain battalions in the army swore allegiance to Talend, others to Gav. The two young men met, but only to stare at each other coldly and to promise war instead of peace, and war was fast approaching. Two opposing armies were built up, consisting of weapons, money, horses and elephants, very important in Persia, for they carried on their backs a wickerwork turret from which the archers fired arrows at the enemy. Gav's army began to march against Talend's. All Persia held its breath, awaiting the battle that was to decide its fate.

The battle was fought. Both armies had the same number of foot soldiers, horsemen, standard bearers and elephants. It was a terrible massacre. Neither of the brothers wanted the other to die. In spite of everything, the brothers felt the call of the family tie. Indeed, each had given an order that, if the soldiers found they were about to kill the enemy leader, they were to stop and warn him instead by shouting,

"Watch out, King!" The conflict lasted for a long time, until Gav's troops were overcome and Talend found himself with only a few soldiers to defend him. Then, a little later, quite alone, he found himself surrounded on all sides by Gav's turreted elephants, slowly advancing on him. No arrows were fired on the prince, he turned this way and that, searching for a way to escape, but his heart failed at that moment and he fell dead to the ground.

High in the palace tower, the Queen had watched the battle with sorrow in her heart, knowing full well that she was, at that moment, losing one of her sons. But which one? It didn't matter. She loved them both equally. When she saw that the dust had settled on the distant plain and the cries of battle had died away, the Queen came down from the tower and rushed through the palace to meet those returning from the field. She stopped in her tracks. Her son Gav, his clothes in tatters and splashed with blood, staggered sadly towards her.

"Talend?" stammered the Queen. Gav shook his head,

"Oh, mother," he said, "my brother Talend is dead."

"Dead! Did you kill him?"

"Oh, no, mother!" exclaimed Gav. "I would never have done such a thing."

"But you ordered his death!" exclaimed the Queen. The young man then knelt before her and, taking the hem of her dress in his hand, said,

"Mother, I swear nobody was responsible for my brother's death. He died, but not violently."

"I shall never believe that is the truth," wept the Queen. But Gav said,

"I shall prove that it is." He then thought of a way to show his mother how the battle had been fought. First of all, he asked a carpenter to make him a board, as flat as the plain. Then to mark the positions and manoeuvres of the two armies, the board was divided into white and black squares. A wood carver made him a miniature army of foot soldiers, a king, standard bearers, knights and towers, to take the place of the elephants and their turrets. When everything was ready, Gav called the Queen and, moving one piece at a time, acted out the various stages of battle.

"You see, mother, my foot soldiers advanced like this, so Talend manoeuvred his like that. Each time my brother was about to be killed, I had the men cry out 'watch out, King,' so that he could reach safety," said Gav.

"In the end, though, my Talend was no longer safe," murmured the Queen. Gav sadly replied,

"That's true. He was surrounded. But I would never have had him killed, mother. It was his heart that gave out. My brother realised he had lost, and so he died." The Queen then said,

"I understand, son, and I forgive you. I feel you'll be a good king for our country. But I wonder why, in a battle between two kings, one must win and the other lose . . ."

The poor Queen kept asking herself the same question for a very long time. She would sit all day long beside the little battlefield moving the pieces, foot soldiers, standard bearers and towers, always trying to save the King. In the end, she understood that, as in make-believe, so it is in real life, when there is a fight to the last, one of the opponents must fall, just as her son Talend had fallen.

One day, they found the poor Queen dead on what was, by then, known as the chessboard. That is how chess originated. Nowadays it is a peaceful contest that recalls a real-life battle. Today it is fun, but then it caused a poor mother who saw her sons fight against each other, sadness and suffering . . .

BLUEBEARD

Once upon a time . . . in the fair land of France, there lived a very rich and powerful lord, the owner of estates, farms and a great splendid castle, and his name was Bluebeard. This wasn't his real name, it was a nickname, due to the fact he had a long shaggy black beard with glints of blue in it. He was very handsome and charming, but, if the truth be told, there was something about him that made you feel respect, and a little uneasy . . .

Bluebeard often went away to war, and when he did, he left

his wife in charge of the castle . . . He had had lots of wives, all young, pretty and noble. As bad luck would have it, one after the other, they had all died, and so the noble lord was forever getting married again.

"Sire," someone would ask now and again, "what did your wives die of?"

"Hah, my friend," Bluebeard would reply, "one died of smallpox, one of a hidden sickness, another of a high fever, another of a terrible infection . . . Ah, I'm very unlucky, and they're unlucky too! They're all buried in the castle chapel," he added. Nobody found anything strange about that. Nor did the sweet and beautiful young girl that Bluebeard took as a wife think it strange either. She went to the castle accompanied by her sister Anna, who said:

"Oh, aren't you lucky marrying a lord like Bluebeard?"

"He really is very nice . . . and when you're close, his beard doesn't look as blue as folk say!" said the bride, and the two sisters giggled delightedly. Poor souls! They had no idea what lay in store for them! . . .

A month or so later, Bluebeard had the carriage brought round and said to his wife, "Darling, I must leave you for a few weeks. But keep cheerful during that time, invite whoever you like and look after the castle. Here," he added, handing his bride a bunch of keys, "you'll need these, the keys of the safe, the armoury and the library keys, and this one, which opens all the room doors. Now, this little key here," and he pointed to a key that was much smaller than the others, "opens the little room at the end of the great ground floor corridor. Take your friends wherever you want, open any door you like, but not this one! Is that quite clear?" repeated Bluebeard. "Not this one! Nobody at all is allowed to enter that little room. And if you ever did go into it, I would go into such a terrible rage that it's better that you don't!"

"Don't worry, husband," said Bluebeard's wife as she took the keys, "I'll do as you say." After giving her a hug, Bluebeard got into his carriage, whipped up the horses and off he went.

The days went by. The young girl invited her friends to the castle and showed them round all the rooms except the one at the end of the corridor.

"Why shouldn't I see inside the little room? Why? Why is it forbidden?" Well, she thought about it so much that she ended up bursting with curiosity, until one day she opened the door and walked into the little room . . . Of all the ghastly horrors! Inside, hanging on the walls were the bodies of Bluebeard's wives; he had strangled them all with his own hands!

Terror stricken, the girl ran out of the room, but the bunch of keys slipped from her grasp. She picked them up without a glance and hurried to her own room, her heart thumping wildly in her chest. Horrors! She was living in a castle of the dead! So that is what had happened to Bluebeard's other wives!

The girl summoned up her courage and she noticed that one of the keys – the very key to the little room – was stained with blood.

"I must wipe it clean, before my husband comes back!" she said to herself. But try as she would, the blood stain wouldn't wash away. She washed, she scrubbed and she rinsed it; all in vain, for the key was still red. That very evening, Bluebeard came home. Just imagine the state his poor wife was in!

Bluebeard did not ask his wife for the keys that same evening, but he remarked:

"You look a little upset, darling. Has anything nasty happened?"

"Oh, no! No!"

"Are you sorry I came back so soon?"

"Oh, no! I'm delighted!" But that night, the bride didn't sleep a wink. Next day, Bluebeard said:

"Darling, give me back the keys," and his wife hurriedly did so. Bluebeard remarked: "There's one missing, the key to the little room!"

"Is there?" said the young girl, shaking,

"I must have left it in my room!"

"All right, go and get it." But when Bluebeard's wife put the key into his hand, Bluebeard turned white and in a deep hoarse voice demanded:

"Why is this key stained with blood?"

"I don't know . . ." stammered his wife.

"You know very well!" he retorted. "You went into the little room, didn't you? Well, you'll go back again, this time for good, along with the other ladies in there. You must die!"

"Oh no! I pray you!"

"You must die!" he repeated. Just then, there was a knock at the door and Anna, Bluebeard's wife's sister, entered the castle.

"Good morning," she said, "you seem rather pale."

"Not at all, we're quite well," replied Bluebeard. His wife whispered in his ear:

"Please, please give me ten minutes to live!" Bluebeard replied:

"No more than ten!" The girl ran to her sister Anna who had gone up to one of the towers and asked her,

"Anna, do you see our brothers coming? They promised they would come and see me today!" But Anna replied:

"No, I don't see anyone. What's wrong? You look agitated"

"Anna, please," said the shaken girl, "look again! Are you sure you can't see someone?"

"No," said her sister, "only one or two peasants." Just then the voice of Bluebeard boomed up to them:

"Wife, your time is up! Come here!"

"I'm coming!" she called, but then said to her sister: "Oh Anna, aren't our brothers coming? . . ."

"No," replied Anna. Again Bluebeard shouted up.

"Come down at once! Or I'll come up!" Trembling like a leaf, his wife went downstairs. Bluebeard was clutching a big knife and he grabbed his bride by the hair . . .

"Sister, I can see two horsemen coming!" called out Anna from the tower that very moment. Bluebeard made a horrible face:

"They too will die!" His wife knelt to implore:

"Please, please don't kill me. I'll never tell anyone what I saw! I'll never say a word!"

"Yes, you'll never say a word for eternity!" snarled Bluebeard, raising the knife. The poor girl screamed:

"Have pity on me!" But he fiercely replied:

"No! You must die!" He was about to bring the knife down on the girl's delicate neck, when two young men burst into the room: a dragoon and a musketeer. They were his wife's brothers.

Drawing their swords, they leapt towards Bluebeard, who tried to flee up some stairs, but was caught and killed. And that was the end of the sad story. Bluebeard's poor wives were given a Christian burial, the castle was completely renovated and the young widow, some time later, married a good and honest young man, who helped her to forget her terrible adventure. And that young lady completely lost all her sense of curiosity . . .

Once upon a time . . .

. . . there lived a little tin soldier. Even though he had been made just like all other tin soldiers, he had a heart and feelings. Here is the extraordinary story of his adventures.

THE TIN SOLDIER

Once upon a time . . . there lived a child who had a lot of toys. The child kept his toys in his room and spent many happy hours everyday playing with them. One of his favourite games was the battle with the tin soldiers. He arranged the little toy soldiers in their respective ranks and fought imaginary battles.

When the boy received the soldiers, as a present, he noticed that one of them had been made, by mistake, with just one leg. Despite the missing limb, the boy placed the little mutilated soldier in the front lines, encouraging him to be the most valorous of all the little soldiers. The child did not know that, at night, the toys became animated and talked between themselves.

It often happened that, when lining up the soldiers after playing with them, the little boy would forget about the little tin soldier without a leg and left him with all the other toys. It was thus that the little metal soldier got to talk to a pretty tin ballerina.

A great friendship was born between the two, and pretty soon the little soldier fell in love with the ballerina. But the nights went by quickly, and he did not find the courage to declare his love to her. When the child played with the soldiers and positioned him in the front lines, the little soldier hoped that the ballerina would notice his courage in battle. And in the evening, when the ballerina asked the soldier if he had been afraid, he proudly answered, "No."

But the loving stares and sighs of the little soldier did not go unnoticed by the jack-in-the-box. One night, the jack-in-the-box said to the little soldier: "Hey you! Don't look at the ballerina like that!" The poor little soldier was confused and he blushed, but the kind ballerina cheered him up.

"Don't listen to him, he is ugly and jealous. I am very happy to talk to you," she said blushing too. The two little tin figurines were both too shy to speak of their love.

One day they were separated. The boy picked up the tin soldier and placed him on the window-sill.

"You stay here and watch for the enemy," he said. Then the boy played inside with the other soliders.

It was summer and in the days that followed the soldier remained on the window-sill. But one afternoon there was a sudden storm and a strong wind shook the windows. The little soldier fell head first off the window-sill. His bayonet stuck into the ground. It kept raining and storming and pretty soon the rain formed big puddles and the gutters were full. A group of boys in the nearby school waited for the storm to end and when it stopped raining hard they ran outdoors.

Joking and laughing, the boys hopped over the bigger puddles while two of them cautiously walked next to the wall so that the sprinkling rain wouldn't wet them. These two boys noticed the little tin soldier stuck in the sodden earth.

"Too bad he has just one leg. Otherwise, I'd take him home with me," one of the boys said. The other boy picked him up and put him in his pocket.

"Let's take him anyway," he said. "We could use him for something." On the other side of the street, the gutter was overflowing and the current carried a little paper boat.

"Let's put the little soldier in the boat and make him a sailor," said the boy who had picked up the tin soldier. And so the little soldier became a sailor.

The whirling gutter flowed into a sewer and the little
boat was carried down the drain. The water in the
underground sewage was deep and muddy. Big rats
gnashed their teeth as the vessel and its unusual passenger
flowed by. The boat was soaked and about to sink. But the
little soldier, who had faced far greater dangers in battle,
was not afraid. The water of the sewer then flowed into the

river and the little boat, now overturned, was swept by the high waves. The little tin soldier realized his end was near. After the paper boat was wrecked, he sank in deep waters. A thousand thoughts went through the little soldier's mind, but one in particular anguished him:

"I will never see my sweet little ballerina again!" But a huge mouth swallowed the little tin soldier and, once again, his destiny took an unexpected turn.

The little soldier found himself in the stomach of a large fish who had been lured by the glittering colours of his uniform. The fish, however, did not even have time to digest his meal because, shortly after having swallowed the soldier, he was caught in the net of a fisherman. Shortly after, the gasping fish ended up in a big basket and was brought to the market.

Meanwhile, a cook was on her way to the market. She worked in the very same house where the little soldier used to live.

"This fish will be perfect for tonight's guests," the cook said when she saw the big fish on the fish market's counter. The fish ended up in the kitchen and when the cook slit its belly to clean it she found the little tin soldier.

"This looks like one of our boy's toy soldiers . . ." she thought, and ran to the boy to show him her discovery.

"That's right, it's my soldier!" the little boy cheered, when he recognized the soldier with the missing leg.

"I wonder how he got into the fish's belly? Poor soldier, he must have gone through a lot of trouble since he fell off the window-sill!" The little boy placed the soldier on the mantle, right next to his sister's ballerina.

The amazing ways of destiny had once again reunited the two lovers. The little soldier and the ballerina were very happy to be close to each other. At night they talked about what had happened after their separation. But the ill disposition of fate had another surprise in store for them.

One day a sudden gust of wind lifted the heavy drape of the window and hit the ballerina, who fell into the fireplace. The little soldier saw his friend fall into the fireplace and he was frightened. He knew a fire was lit because he could feel its warmth. He was desperate, conscious of not being able to do anything to save the ballerina. In fact, fire is the greatest enemy of tin figurines because it melts metals. Rocking back and forth on his one leg, the little soldier tried to move the metal base under his feet that held him in place.

He kept trying to move until he fell into the fire as well. The two figurines were reunited in their misfortune. They were so close to each other now, that their metal bases began melting together. The tin of one base melted with the metal of the other, and the metal strangely moulded into the shape of a heart. As their bodies were about to begin melting as well, the little boy went by the fireplace and saw the two little figurines enveloped by the flames and moved them away from the blaze with his foot.

Ever since then the soldier and the ballerina have been melted close to each other, sharing their destiny and a common base shaped like a heart.

THE ELVES AND THE SHOEMAKER

Once upon a time there lived a poor shoemaker. He lived in misery because as he grew old he could not see all that well anymore and, consequently he could not work like he used to.

One night he went to bed sad, without finishing a repair job he had begun. In the morning he found the job done.

During the day he set out all the tools and material necessary to make a new pair of shoes for a rich customer.

"Tomorrow morning, when it will be sunny and bright, I will begin working on them," he thought. But the morning after, instead of the leather he had left the night before, the shoemaker was very surprised to find a beautiful pair of brand new shoes. Later on in the day, the customer went by the shop to see how his new shoes were coming along. When he found a very nice pair of shoes ready, he was very happy and paid the shoemaker twice the price they had agreed upon

The shoemaker was very confused and wondered what had happened. That night, he left out some more leather and the next morning he found another shiny and perfect pair of new

shoes. These shoes were sold at an even higher price. Now the shoemaker left out leather and tools to his mysterious helper every night, and, every morning, he found a new pair of shoes. Pretty soon, the shoemaker was able to save a good sum of money. When the shoemaker's wife noticed all the money the shoemaker had saved, she grew suspicious and demanded an explanation. When she was informed of the unusual nocturnal occurrences, she proposed:

"Let's wait until nightfall. We will hide and find out what's happening."

And so the shoemaker and his wife hid and, around midnight, saw two elves sneak into the shoemaker's shop. The quick and skilled elves made a new pair of shoes in a flash. It was winter and the elves, dressed in ragged clothes, shivered while they worked.

"Poor fellows! They must be very cold," the shoemaker's wife whispered to her husband. "Tomorrow I will make them two heavy wool jackets. That way they will be warmer and maybe, instead of one pair of shoes, they will make two!"

The following midnight, next to the leather, the two elves found two elegant red jackets with gold buttons. They put on the jackets and were very happy. They danced shouting:

"What beautiful jackets! We'll never be cold again." But when one of the elves said:

"Let's get to work now," the other answered:

"Work? What for? With two jackets like these we are rich. We will never have to work again."

The two elves left the shop of the astonished shoemaker and his even more puzzled wife and were never seen again.

THE TAIL OF THE BEAR

Once upon a time there lived a fisherman who earned a living selling fish, making his rounds to the customers on a horse-drawn cart loaded with his catch of the day.

One cold winter day, while the fisherman was crossing the woods, a fox smelled the fish and began following the cart at a close distance. The fisherman kept his trout in long wicker baskets and the sight of the fish made the fox's mouth water. The fox, however, was reluctant to jump on the cart to steal a fish because the fisherman had a long whip that he cracked from time to time to spur on the horse. But the smell of fresh fish was so enticing that the fox overcame her fear of the whip, leapt on to the cart and with a quick blow of her paw, dropped a wicker basket on the snow. The fisherman did not notice anything and continued his journey undisturbed.

The fox was very happy. She opened the basket and got ready to enjoy her meal. She was about to taste the first bite when a bear appeared.

"Where did you get all that marvellous trout?" the big bear asked with a hungry look on its face.

"I've been fishing," the fox answered, unperturbed.

"Fishing? How? The lake is frozen over," the bear said, incredulously. "How did you manage to fish?"

The fox was aware that, unless she could get rid of the bear with some kind of excuse, she would have had to share her fish. But the only plausible answer she could come up with was:

"I fished with my tail."

"With your tail?" said the bear, who was even more astonished.

"Sure, with my tail. I made a hole in the ice, I dropped my tail in the water and when I felt a bite I pulled it out and a fish was stuck on its end," the fox told the bear. The bear touched his tail and his mouth began watering. He said:

"Thanks for the tip. I'm going fishing too."

The lake was not too far away, but the ice was very thick and the bear had a hard time making a hole in it. Finally, his long claws got the job done. As time went by and evening approached, it got colder and colder. The bear shivered but he kept sitting by the hole with his tail in the water. No fish had bitten yet.

The bear was very cold and the water of the lake began freezing again around his tail. It was then that the bear felt something like a bite on the end of his frozen tail. The bear pulled with all his strength, heard something tear and at the same time felt a very sharp pain. He turned around to find out what kind of fish he had caught, and right then he realized that his tail, trapped in the ice, had been torn off.

Ever since then, bears have had a little stump instead of a long and thick tail.

A SHREWD FARMER'S STORY

Once upon a time there lived a farmer who worked far from his home in the fields of a rich baron.

In the past, gangs of bandits hid in the mountains rising behind the plain but the emperor had sent his soldiers to find and kill the thieves and now the area was safe and quiet. Every once in a while, however, old weapons from past battles could be found in the fields.

While he was chopping a stump one day, the farmer found a bag full of gold. The farmer had only ever seen silver coins in his life, and he was so astonished to find all that gold, that when he started walking home it was already dark. On his way home, the farmer thought about the problems that this sudden wealth could cause him.

First of all, everything found on the baron's territory belonged to the baron. By law, the farmer had to hand the gold over to the baron. The farmer decided that it was much more fair for him to keep the treasure because he was very poor, rather than giving it to the baron who already had a lot of money. He realized the risk he would run if anyone found out about his luck. He would never tell anyone, of course, but his wife had a reputation for talking too much and she would never keep a secret. Sooner or later he would end up in jail.

He thought the problem over and over until he found a solution. Before getting home he left the bag full of gold in a bush next to some pine trees and the day after, instead of going to work, he went by the village to buy a few nice trout, some doughnuts and a rabbit. In the afternoon he went home and said to his wife:

"Get your wicker basket and come with me. Yesterday it rained and the wood is full of mushrooms. We must get to them before someone else does!" The wife, who loved mushrooms, picked up her basket and followed her husband. When they got to the woods the farmer ran to his wife shouting:

"Look! Look! We have found a doughnut tree!" and he showed her the branches he had previously loaded with doughnuts.

The wife was astonished but she was even more puzzled when, instead of mushrooms, she found trout in the grass. The farmer laughed happily.

"Today is our lucky day! My grandfather said that everyone has one lucky day. We might even find a treasure!" In addition to being a gossip, the farmer's wife was also a sucker. So she believed her husband and repeated, while looking around: "This is our lucky day, this is our lucky day."

The basket of the woman was full of fish by now. When she and her husband reached the banks the farmer ran ahead of her, looked into the thicket and said:

"Yesterday I laid out my nets and I want to check whether I've caught any fish or shrimps." A few minutes later the wife heard the husband shout:

"Run and see what I've caught! What extraordinary luck! I've fished a rabbit!" They were walking back home and the wife kept talking excitedly about the great dinner with the doughnuts, the fish and the rabbit. The husband said: "Let's go by the wood again. We could find other doughnuts!"

They went to the spot where the farmer had hidden his gold coins. The farmer pretended to find something.

"Look over here! There's a strange bag and . . . it's full of gold! This is an enchanted forest. We found the doughnuts on the trees, then we found the trout in the grass and now . . . gold." The poor woman was so excited that tears filled her eyes. She could not utter another word and gulped as she touched the shiny coins.

At home, after dinner, neither of the two could fall asleep. The farmer and his wife kept getting up to look over the treasure they had hidden in an old boot. The day after the farmer went back to work, but first said to his wife:

"Don't tell anybody about what happened yesterday." And he repeated the same recommendation every day after that. Pretty soon, however, the entire village had heard about the treasure. The farmer and his wife were called by the baron and when they went in to see him the farmer tried to stand behind his wife. His

wife, at the request of the baron, spoke first of the doughnuts, then of the trout on the grass and lastly of the rabbit in the river. Meanwhile, behind her, the husband kept tapping his forehead with his finger and gesticulating to the baron. The baron began looking at the woman with pity.

"And then I bet you found a treasure, too."

"That's right, Sir!" the woman said. The baron turned to the farmer and, tapping his finger on his forehead sympathetically said:

"I see what you mean. Unfortunately, I have the same problem with my wife . . ."

The farmers were sent home and no one believed their story. And so the shrewd farmer didn't go to jail and spent his money wisely.

JACK AND THE BEANSTALK

Once upon a time there was a poor widow who lived with her son Jack in a little house. Their wealth consisted solely of a milking cow. When the cow had grown too old, the mother sent Jack to sell it. On his way to the market, the boy met a stranger.

"I will give you five magic beans for your cow," the stranger offered. Jack was unsure and hesitated for a while but then, enticed by the idea of such an extraordinary deal, he decided to accept. When he returned home, his mother was furious and reprimanded him sternly:

"You fool! What have you done? We needed the money to buy a calf. Now we don't have anything and we are even poorer." Jack felt guilty and sad.

"Only a fool would exchange a cow for five beans," his mother fumed.

Then, at the height of her exasperation, she threw the five beans out of the window and sent Jack to bed with no dinner.

The morning after, when he stepped outside, Jack saw an amazing sight. A gigantic beanstalk, reaching far into the clouds, had grown overnight.

"The beans must have really been magic," Jack thought happily. Being very curious, the boy climbed the plant and once he reached the top of the stalk he found himself over the clouds.

While looking around in amazement, Jack saw a huge castle of grey stone.

"I wonder who lives there," he thought. Jack was very surprised to see a path leading to the castle. He cautiously stepped on the clouds and, when he saw that they held him up, he walked to the castle. As he stood in front of the huge gate, his curiosity increased. He knocked several times on the gigantic door, but no one came to open it. Jack noticed that the door wasn't locked. With great effort, he was able to push it until it creaked open.

"What are you doing here?" a thundering voice asked. The biggest woman he had ever seen was scowling at him. Jack could only mutter:

"I am lost. May I have something to eat? I am very hungry." The woman, who did not have children, looked at him a little more kindly: "Come in, quick. I will give you a bowl of milk. But be careful because my husband, the ogre, eats children. If you hear him coming, hide at once."

Jack was shaking with fear but, nonetheless, he went inside. The milk the woman gave him was very good and Jack had almost finished drinking it when they heard a tremendous noise. The ogre was home.

"Fee fi fo fum! I smell the blood of an Englishman!" the ogre shouted.

"Hide, quick!" the woman whispered, pushing Jack into the oven.

"Do I smell a child in this room?" the ogre asked suspiciously, sniffing and looking all around.

"A child?" the woman repeated. "You see and hear children everywhere. That's all you ever think about. Sit down and I'll make your dinner." The ogre, still grumbling, filled a jug of wine and drank it all with his dinner.

After having counted again and again all the gold pieces of his treasure, the ogre fell asleep with his feet propped up on the table. After a little while, his thundering snoring echoed throughout the castle. The ogre's wife went to prepare the ogre's bed and Jack, who had sneaked out of the oven, saw the gold pieces on the table and filled a little bag full of them.

"I hope he won't see me, otherwise he'll eat me whole," Jack thought while shivering with fear. Jack's heart was beating faster, not just faster because he feared the ogre but because he was very excited. Thanks to all the gold coins, he and his mother would be rich. Jack ran down the path over the clouds.

Jack arrived at the top of the giant beanstalk and began to descend as quickly as possible, hanging on to the leaves and the branches. When he finally reached the ground, he found his mother waiting for him. The poor woman had been worried sick since his disappearance.

She had been frightened by the giant beanstalk. When she saw Jack come down and then triumphantly hold up the bag full of gold, she burst out crying.

"Where have you been, my son? Do you want me to die worrying? What kind of plant is this? What . . ." Jack cheerfully interrupted her, emptying the contents of the bag before her.

"You see, I did the right thing exchanging that cow for the magic beans. Now I'll tell you the whole story . . ."

And Jack told his mother everything that had happened in detail. In the days that followed, the widow's humble house was made into a comfortable home. The gold pieces were spent to buy a lot of things Jack and his mother never had before. Mother and son were very happy. But as time went by, so did the money. When the last gold piece had been spent, Jack decided to go back to the castle above the clouds. This time the boy went inside through the kitchen and hid once again in the oven. Shortly after, the ogre came in and began to sniff about.

"I smell children," he said to his wife. But since she had seen no one come in, she didn't pay any attention to him.

After dinner, the ogre placed a hen on the table. The hen laid golden eggs. Jack saw the miraculous hen from a crack in the oven door. He waited for the ogre to fall asleep, jumped out of the oven, snatched the hen and ran out of the castle. The hen's squawking, however, woke up the ogre.

"Thief! Thief!" he shouted. But Jack was already far away. Once again, he found his mother anxiously waiting for him at the foot of the beanstalk.

"Is that all you stole? A hen?" she asked Jack, disappointed. But Jack ran, happy, to the court yard.

"Just wait," he said to his mother. As a matter of fact, a little while later the hen laid a golden egg and continued to lay such an egg every single day after that.

By now, Jack and his mother were very wealthy. Their house was completely rebuilt. Teams of carpenters replaced the roof, added new rooms and elegant marble columns. Then they bought paintings, tapestries, Persian rugs, mirrors and many other beautiful furnishings. Their miserable shack was transformed into a luxurious home.

Jack and his mother had not forgotten their previous years of poverty and deprivation. So they chose to welcome any traveller who needed food or shelter. But wealth doesn't always bring happiness. Jack's mother suddenly fell ill or so it seemed. But not one of the many doctors who visited her could discover what her illness was. The woman was sad, ate less and less and showed no interest in life. She rarely smiled, and then only when Jack was near to her. Her son tried to cheer her up, but nothing could save the mother from her slow but inevitable decline. Even a circus's famous clown, who had been invited especially for her entertainment, received only a sad greeting.

Jack was desperate and didn't know what to do. All the hen's gold was not enough to make his mother well again. So he had another idea.

"What if I went back to the ogre's castle? Maybe there I could find the answer," he thought. He shivered with fear thinking about the giant's huge hands and mouth, but the hope of helping his mother encouraged him to face the danger again. One evening he gathered all his courage and climbed once more the giant beanstalk. This time he entered the castle through an open window. He sneaked in the darkness to the kitchen and hid inside a huge pot until the following day. After dinner the ogre went to get his magic harp, an instrument that sang and played marvellous music. While listening to the harp's sweet melody, the ogre fell asleep. In his hiding place, Jack was captivated by the harp's song as well. When he finally heard the ogre snore loudly, he lifted the pot's lid and saw the extraordinary instrument: a golden harp.

He quickly climbed on the table and ran away with the harp in his hands. The instrument woke up the ogre screaming:

"Master, master! Wake up! A thief is taking me away!" The ogre woke up suddenly, was disorientated for a couple of seconds but then realized what was happening and began chasing Jack. The boy ran as fast as he could and the harp kept calling out.

"Shut up! Shut up! If you'll play for me, you'll be happier," Jack kept telling it breathlessly. He finally arrived to where the leafy top of the beanstalk poked through the clouds. Jack crept along the ground and slipped down the stalk quietly. The harp did not make a sound and the ogre didn't see Jack go down the plant. When Jack got down to earth he called to his mother,

"Look what I've brought you!" The harp began to play an enchanting melody and his mother smiled happily.

But up there in the clouds someone else had heard the harp's beautiful song and Jack soon realized with terror that the thick beanstalk was shaking under a very heavy weight. The ogre was coming down to earth!

"Hide the harp and bring me an axe! I must chop down the plant before the ogre gets here," Jack said to his mother. They could already see the ogre's huge boots when the plant and the ogre finally crashed to the ground. The ogre fell down a cliff nearby. The ogre's wife never found out what had happened to her husband and as time passed Jack no longer felt in danger.

The magical sound of the harp cured his mother's sadness and she was once again happy and cheerful. The hen kept on laying golden eggs. Jack's life had gone through a lot of changes since he had accepted the magic beans. But without his courage and his wit, he and his mother could never have found happiness.

THE EMPEROR'S NEW CLOTHES

Once upon a time there lived a vain emperor whose only worry in life was to dress in elegant clothes. He changed clothes almost every hour and loved to show them off to his people.

Word of the Emperor's refined habits spread over his kingdom and beyond. Two scoundrels who had heard of the Emperor's vanity decided to take advantage of it. They introduced themselves at the gates of the palace with a scheme in mind.

"We are two very good tailors and after many years of research we have invented an extraordinary method to weave a cloth so light and fine that it looks invisible. As a matter of fact it is invisible to anyone who is too stupid and incompetent to appreciate its quality."

The chief of the guards heard the scoundrel's strange story and sent for the court chamberlain. The chamberlain notified the prime minister, who ran to the Emperor and disclosed the incredible news. The Emperor's curiosity got the better of him and he decided to see the two scoundrels.

"Besides being invisible, your Highness, this cloth will be woven in colours and patterns created especially for you." The emperor gave the two men a bag of gold coins in exchange for their promise to begin working on the fabric immediately.

"Just tell us what you need to get started and we'll give it to you." The two scoundrels asked for a loom, silk, gold thread and then pretended to begin working. The Emperor thought he had spent his money quite well: in addition to getting a new extraordinary suit, he would discover which of his subjects were ignorant and incompetent. A few days later, he called the old and wise prime minister, who was considered by everyone as a man with common sense.

"Go and see how the work is proceeding," the Emperor told him, "and come back to let me know."

The prime minister was welcomed by the two scoundrels.

"We're almost finished, but we need a lot more gold thread. Here, Excellency! Admire the colours, feel the softness!" The old man bent over the loom and tried to see the fabric that was not there. He felt cold sweat on his forehead.

"I can't see anything," he thought. "If I see nothing, that means I'm stupid! Or, worse, incompetent!" If the prime minister admitted that he didn't see anything, he would be discharged from his office.

"What a marvellous fabric," he said then. "I'll certainly tell the Emperor." The two scoundrels rubbed their hands gleefully. They had almost made it. More thread was requested to finish the work.

Finally, the Emperor received the announcement that the two tailors had come to take all the measurements needed to sew his new suit.

"Come in," the Emperor ordered. Even as they bowed, the two scoundrels pretended to be holding a large roll of fabric.

"Here it is, your Highness, the result of our labour," the scoundrels said. "We have worked night and day but, at last, the most beautiful fabric in the world is ready for you. Look at the colours and feel how fine it is." Of course the Emperor did not see any colours and could not feel any cloth between his fingers. He panicked and felt like fainting. But luckily the throne was right behind him and he sat down. But when he realized that no one could know that he did not see the fabric, he felt better. Nobody could find out he was stupid and incompetent. And the Emperor didn't know that everybody else around him thought and did the very same thing.

The farce continued as the two scoundrels had foreseen it. Once they had taken the measurements, the two began cutting the air with scissors while sewing with their needles an invisible cloth.

"Your Highness, you'll have to take off your clothes to try on your new ones." The two scoundrels draped the new clothes on him and then held up a mirror. The Emperor was embarrassed but since none of his bystanders were, he felt relieved.

"Yes, this is a beautiful suit and it looks very good on me," the Emperor said trying to look comfortable. "You've done a fine job."

"Your Majesty," the prime minister said, "we have a request for you. The people have found out about this extraordinary fabric and they are anxious to see you in your new suit." The Emperor was doubtful about showing himself naked to the people, but then he abandoned his fears. After all, no one would know about it except the ignorant and the incompetent!

"All right," he said. "I will grant the people this privilege." He summoned his carriage and the ceremonial parade was formed. A group of dignitaries walked at the very front of the procession and anxiously scrutinized the faces of the people in the street. All the people had gathered in the main square, pushing and shoving to get a better look. An applause welcomed the regal procession. Everyone wanted to know how stupid or incompetent his or her neighbour was but, as the Emperor passed, a strange murmur rose from the crowd.

Everyone said, loud enough for the others to hear:

"Look at the Emperor's new clothes. They're beautiful!"

"What a marvellous train!"

"And the colours! The colours of that beautiful fabric! I have never seen anything like it in my life." They all tried to conceal their disappointment at not being able to see the clothes, and since nobody was willing to admit his own stupidity and incompetence, they all behaved as the two scoundrels had predicted.

A child, however, who had no important job and could only see things as his eyes showed them to him, went up to the carriage.

"The Emperor is naked," he said.

"Fool!" his father reprimanded, running after him. "Don't talk nonsense!" He grabbed his child and took him away. But the boy's remark, which had been heard by the bystanders, was repeated over and over again until everyone cried:

"The boy is right! The Emperor is naked! It's true!"

The Emperor realized that the people were right but could not admit to that. He though it better to continue the procession under the illusion that anyone who couldn't see his clothes was either stupid or incompetent. And he stood stiffly on his carriage, while behind him a page held his imaginary mantle.

SIX ABLE MEN

Once upon a time there lived a young soldier named Martin who had enlisted in the royal army to fight a war. The war was long but victorious and when the King abandoned the enemy's territory and returned with his troops to the homeland, he left Martin to guard the only bridge on the river that separated the two nations.

"Stay on watch on the bridge," the King ordered. "Don't let any enemy soldier go by." Days and then months passed, and the soldier kept his watch on the bridge. He survived by asking the passers-by for food and, after two years, thought that the authorities had probably forgotten him. He then headed towards the capital, where he would ask the King for all his back pay. His pockets were empty and his only possessions were a pipe, a bit of tobacco and his sword.

A couple of days later he arrived in a valley where a stream crossed his path. A big man with hands as big as hams, large shoulders and a bull's neck was sitting by the stream. The man, who had a strangely soft and kind voice, asked him:

"Would you like to cross the stream?" The soldier couldn't ask for more. The man effortlessly uprooted a huge tree and laid it across the stream. Martin offered the man some of his tobacco in return and when he found out that the man had nothing to do, Martin asked him to come along.

"You'll see all the things we can do together!"

They had just begun walking away when they met a hunter who was aiming his rifle at a faraway hill.

"What are you aiming at?"

"Do you see that cobweb on that tree on top of the hill?" the hunter asked. "I want to get the spider!" The hunter shot and

when the three men got to the top of the hill they found a big
hole in the middle of the cobweb and no more spider. Martin had
never seen anyone shoot that well and he asked the hunter to
join them.

"Come with us and you'll be in luck!" The three men walked
and walked until they arrived at a windmill. The wheel of the mill
was turning even though there was no wind. The men were
puzzled but further up the road they found a fat man sitting on a
tree stump. The man was blowing through one of his nostrils in
the mill's direction. The fat man explained to the three amazed
fellow travellers that his strength was such that he could sneeze

up a hurricane. The soldier convinced him to follow them. As they approached the city, they were approached by a man who hopped about with his legs tied together.

"Who tied you up?" they asked in unison.

"I did it myself," the man, who was very young and very thin, answered. "If I untied myself I would run as fast as the wind and would not enjoy the sights." And so it was that even this character, nicknamed Fastfoot by the others, joined the group.

But the surprises of that extraordinary day were far from over. A little man with a round face sat under a tree. He held his hat over his left ear. "If I straighten my hat," he explained, "I will freeze everything around me." Naturally, everybody took his word for it and the stranger was asked to join the group. The bizarre company finally arrived at the city. A public notice was hung outside the city walls. The princess announced that whoever would beat her in a race could marry her.

The soldier dusted his uniform, cleaned himself up after the long trip and ran to the palace. He wanted to challenge the princess but said that one of his servants would run in his place. The princess accepted his challenge. The morning after, at the starting line, Fastfoot untied his legs and took off like a rocket. Each one of the contestants had a jug that had to be filled at a nearby stream and brought back full to the finish line. On his way back, Fastfoot stopped to pick a flower and after carefully setting the jug on the ground and realizing that the princess was still far away, he decided to lie down and rest for a while. Unfortunately, he fell asleep.

Later on, when the princess caught up with him and saw that he had fallen asleep, she kicked down his jug and ran away. She was sure of her victory. From far away the sharp sighted hunter shot and hit a spot near Fastfoot's ear. Fastfoot woke up all of a sudden and saw the princess approaching the finish line. He quickly ran back to the stream, filled the jug and reached the finish line as fast as lightning. The King was furious. He would never let his daughter marry a miserable soldier.

He invited the unsuspecting Martin to the palace. Martin told him about his two years watching over the river, which made the King ever angrier. The King, however, pretended to feel guilty and invited the soldier and his friends to a banquet in a strange dining room. In fact the dining room was lined with iron walls and was built over a huge furnace. The King ordered his men to seal the dining room's door and to light the furnace. Then he proceeded to watch the slow death of the group through an unbreakable glass. The six men began eating but suddenly felt the floor grow very hot, while the room's temperature rapidly increased.

But Martin did not lose his head. He straightened the hat of the round faced little man and pretty soon they were all shivering from the cold. The King uselessly urged his men to throw more and more wood in the furnace, but the soldier and his friends had found a remedy to the King's wickedness. No one had ever come out of this torture chamber alive, but this time the King had to accept defeat, even though he was still determined not to let his

daughter go. He offered the soldier a large sum of money as long as he gave up the wedding.

"I will fill you a bag of gold and other riches if you forget the wedding."

"That's fine with me," Martin said, "and I accept your offer but as long as I pick the bag and the man who will carry it away." The poor King was unaware of the strength of one of the six friends. When he began filling the sack, all of his gold was not enough to fill it. Martin and his friends were rich. When they left court, the King had become very poor.

The monarch lost his temper and realized the soldier had fooled him. He called the army commander and ordered two battalions to chase Martin. "Bring them back dead or alive and at all costs!" Later on, the soldiers caught up with the six young men and surrounded them.

"Give us back the gold and surrender," they demanded. But the fattest of the men began blowing so hard that horses and soldiers were carried away. In just a few minutes the wounded soldiers were scattered all over the plain and the battalions were no longer a threat to the six extraordinary friends who continued their journey.

Then they divided the gold and jewels in equal parts and each one of them went his own separate way. Martin crossed the bridge where he had been on watch for so long without any reward and never turned back again.

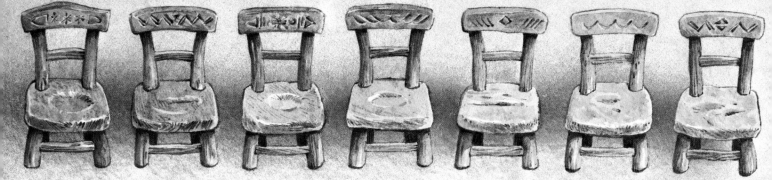

THE SEVEN CROWS

Once upon a time there was, far away amid high mountains, a green valley. The valley was crossed by a clear stream and a woodsman had built his stone house on its shore.

The woodsman was married and had seven sons and one daughter. He often had to travel from home to work and his wife had a hard time bringing up the children alone. The daughter did not cause her any trouble because she was kind, pretty and helpful. But the boys were the cause of her problems because they were rude, disobedient and quarrelsome. They had no respect for their mother and she was very worried for them.

When the husband returned home tired after a week's hard work, the poor wife couldn't bring herself to tell him of the sons' mischievous behaviour because she didn't want to worry him further. The woman kept her sorrow to herself not realizing that by doing so her sons would only get worse and worse. As a matter of fact, when their father was not home to punish them, the boys kept on taking advantage of the situation which continued to get worse.

Their sister suffered most because she loved her brothers even if they were wicked, but she loved her mother especially. Being the youngest, however, none of the brothers paid any attention to her reprimands.

One day the seven boys got into the biggest trouble yet. In the woods grew a dangerous grass which causes the animals stomachs to swell. The woodsman had always told his sons to make sure that their goats never ate any. The cruel boys filled a bag with the grass and then mixed it in with the animals' food. Later on the goats and the cow fell ill, their bellies swelled and ached and they could not stand up.

"We won't have any more milk! We won't be able to make any cheese!" the mother cried desperately. "How will we survive?" The sons laughed maliciously and did not realize the evil they had done until the woman, at the height of her desperation, cried:

"I wish you were crows rather than sons of mine!" When she spoke these words, a mysterious cloud overshadowed the sun, it was suddenly very chilly and the boys turned into seven big crows that flew away croaking.

The woman was so frightened and felt such regret that she fainted. When the father came back from work the day after, he found out the truth and was very upset. Nevertheless he tried to comfort his wife, telling her she was not to blame for the terrible wish that had been fulfilled. But the house was filled with sadness and despair.

A long time passed and the little girl grew older. She still remembered her brothers and rarely smiled. One day she asked her mother's permission to go and look for them.

"I will find them, I feel it. I feel I have to go and that they are expecting me. Let me go, Mother, and give me your blessing." The mother could not resist her daughter's pleas and the little girl left home with a little bundle of provisions. She walked for two days through the woods, climbing towards the mountains. Pretty soon she had no more food, her clothes were torn and she was cold and tired.

The third day, at dawn, she saw a strange little cottage in the mist. Something attracted her to the house even though it had a gloomy and uninviting appearance. When she was inside the house she found a little table with seven bowls on it and her heart beat very fast . . . maybe she had found what she was looking for. There was a large pot full of wheat and oats on the fire.

The little girl was very hungry and so she poured a bit of food in a bowl and ate it avidly. Then she went upstairs and found a little bedroom with seven little beds, each one with a different blanket. With tears in her eyes, the little girl realized she had finally found her brothers. Exhausted by the trip and the commotion, the little girl lay down on a bed and fell asleep.

Later on, seven chattering crows pushed open the front door and sat around the kitchen table.

"Someone has eaten some of our soup," one of the crows said after finding the dirty bowl.

"But who would ever come up here?" answered another.

"We're condemned to be alone on these mountains forever."

"Nobody will ever come to look for us." When they finished eating, the crows pulled on their sleeping caps, went upstairs and found the little girl in one of their beds.

"But this is . . ." one of the crows said, after delicately touching her braid with his beak.

"That's right, this is . . . our sister," they said all together. At that moment the little girl opened her eyes and when she saw herself surrounded by the big and ugly birds, she was frightened. But out of one ugly beak spoke a kind voice:

"Are you our sister?" The little girl got up and opened her arms:

"I've found you! I've found you! We're together again at last!" The seven crows looked at her sadly and one said:

"Don't we frighten and disgust you?" The girl hugged every one of them.

"I love you very much and even if you've turned into crows you're still my brothers." When they heard this, the crows were moved and began crying.

"Why don't you come back home with me?" she asked.

"We would like very much to come back," they all answered together, "and we regret our evil ways. But how can we show ourselves to our parents like this?"

"Mother would accept you all the same, I am sure of it. She keeps crying and thinking of you," the little girl answered.

The little girl insisted and convinced her brothers to come home with her.

"There's no need to walk back up and down the mountains like you did. We will fly there and carry you," they said. As they were about to leave, the youngest brother said,

"Wait a minute! Let's bring Mother all the sparkling stones we found as a present."

"They are really beautiful," the little girl said when she saw the bag with her brothers' treasure.

"Do you like them? They might be precious, you know. When we crows see something sparkle, we cannot help ourselves and take it."

"This one sparkles more than the rest, maybe it's a diamond." They finally left. The world was very different from above. At first the little girl was scared, but the seven crows held her firmly and flew safely. Then they saw the valley, the stream and the little house where they were born. The courtyard was deserted and when they landed the little girl said,

"You wait here and I'll go and call Mother."

She silently went into the kitchen and saw the poor woman leaning on the table and weeping. She hugged her and kissed her saying,

"Mother I'm back and I have a big surprise for you."

"You're here at last! I thought I'd lost you forever." The poor woman was so happy and moved that she didn't know whether to laugh or to cry. In the courtyard she found the crows.

"My poor sons! I missed you so much. I am so sorry to have uttered that curse. A mother should never say such things against her children."

"We regret all we have done too. We very much regret our wickedness." They were all crying over the past when, suddenly, another miracle occurred. The seven brothers became boys again. The father, who had heard voices, ran out of the house.

"Thank God I can see my children again," he cried as he hugged his sons and his daughter.

The years passed and the crows' hats became the only memory of this moving story.

The stones the crows had brought to their mother turned out to be precious after all, and the treasure allowed the family to live a better future.

Once upon a time . . .

. . . in the Far East lived a boy called Aladdin. This is the tale of Aladdin and a magic lamp which, even today, we would all love to discover . . .

THE ADVENTURES OF ALADDIN

Once upon a time . . . a widow had an only son whose name was Aladdin. They were very poor and lived from hand to mouth, though Aladdin did what he could to earn some pennies, by picking bananas in faraway places.

One day, as he was looking for wild figs in a grove some way from the town,

Aladdin met a mysterious stranger. This smartly dressed dark-eyed man with a trim black beard and a splendid sapphire in his turban, asked Aladdin an unusual question:

"Come here, boy," he ordered. "How would you like to earn a silver penny?"

"A silver penny!" exclaimed Aladdin. "Sir, I'd do anything for that kind of payment."

"I'm not going to ask you to do much. Just go down that manhole. I'm much too big to squeeze through myself. If you do as I ask, you'll have your reward." The stranger helped Aladdin lift the manhole cover, for it was very heavy. Slim and agile as he was, the boy easily went down. His feet touched stone and he carefully made his way down some steps . . . and found himself in a large chamber. It seemed to sparkle, though dimly lit by the flickering light of an old oil lamp. When Aladdin's eyes became used to the gloom, he saw a wonderful sight: trees dripping with glittering jewels, pots of gold and caskets full of priceless gems. Thousands of precious objects lay scattered about. It was a treasure trove! Unable to believe his eyes, Aladdin was standing dazed when he heard a shout behind him.

"The lamp! Put out the flame and bring me the lamp!" Surprised and suspicious, for why should the stranger, out of all such a treasure want only an old lamp, Aladdin wondered. Perhaps he was a wizard. He decided to be on his guard. Picking up the lamp, he retraced his steps up to the entrance.

"Give me the lamp," urged the wizard, impatiently. "Hand it over," he began to shout, thrusting out his arm to grab it, but Aladdin cautiously drew back.

"I'll leave you down there forever if you don't give me the lamp!" the wizard declared.

"Let me out first . . ."

"Too bad for you," snapped the stranger, slamming down the manhole cover, never noticing that, as he did so, a ring slid off his finger. A terrified Aladdin was left in pitch darkness, wondering what the wizard would do next. Then he trod on the ring. Aimlessly putting it on his finger, he twisted it round and round. Suddenly the room was flooded with a rosy light and a great genie with clasped hands appeared on a cloud.

"At your command, sire," said the genie.

Now astounded, Aladdin could only stammer
"I want to go home!" In a flash he was
back in his own home, though the door
was tightly shut.

"How did you get in?" called his mother
from the kitchen stove, the minute she set
eyes on him. Excitedly, her son told her of
his adventures.

"Where's the silver coin?" his mother
asked. Aladdin clapped a hand to his
brow. For all he had brought home was
the old oil lamp. "Oh, mother! I'm so
sorry. This is all I've got."

"Well, let's hope it works. It's so dirty
. . ." and the widow began to rub the lamp.

Suddenly out shot another genie, in a cloud of smoke.

"You've set me free, after centuries! I was a prisoner in the
lamp, waiting to be freed by someone rubbing it. Now, I'm your
obedient servant. Tell me your wishes." And the genie bowed
respectfully, awaiting Aladdin's orders. The boy and his mother
gaped wordlessly at this incredible apparition, then the genie said
with a hint of impatience in his voice.
"I'm here at your command. Tell me what you want. Anything
you like!" Aladdin gulped, then said:

"Bring us . . . bring . . ." His mother not having yet begun to
cook the dinner, went on to say: ". . . a lovely big meal."

From that day on, the widow and her son had everything they could wish for: food, clothes and a fine home, for the genie of the lamp granted them everything they asked him. Aladdin grew into a tall handsome young man and his mother felt that he ought to find himself a wife, sooner or later.

One day, as he left the market, Aladdin happened to see the Sultan's daughter Halima in her sedan chair being carried through the streets. He only caught a fleeting glimpse of the princess, but it was enough for him to want to marry her.

Aladdin told his mother and she quickly said:

"I'll ask the Sultan for his daughter's hand. He'll never be able to refuse. Wait and see!"

And indeed, the Sultan was easily persuaded by a casket full of big diamonds to admit the widow to the palace. However, when he learned why she had come, he told the widow that her son must bring proof of his power and riches. This was mostly the Chamberlain's idea, for he himself was eager to marry the beautiful black-eyed Sultan's daughter.

"If Aladdin wants to marry Halima," said the Sultan, "he must send me forty slaves tomorrow. Every slave must bring a box of precious stones. And forty Arab warriors must escort this treasure."

Aladdin's mother went sadly home. The genie of the magic lamp had already worked wonders, but nothing like this. Aladdin however, when he heard the news, was not at all dismayed. He picked up the lamp, rubbed it harder than ever and told the genie what he required. The genie simply clapped his hands three times. Forty slaves magically appeared, carrying the gemstones, together with their escort of forty Arab warriors. When he saw all this the next day, the Sultan was taken aback. He never imagined such wealth could exist. Just as he was about to accept Aladdin as his daughter's bridegroom, the envious Chamberlain broke in with a question.

"Where will they live?" he asked. The Sultan pondered for a moment, then allowing greed to get the better of him, he told Aladdin to build a great, splendid palace for Halima. Aladdin went straight home and, in what was once a wilderness the genie built him a palace. The last

obstacle had been overcome. The wedding took place with great celebrations and the Sultan was especially happy at finding such a rich and powerful son-in-law.

News of Aladdin's sudden fortune and wealth spread like wildfire, until. . . . one day, a strange merchant stopped beneath the palace window.

"Old lamps for new," he called to the princess, standing on the balcony. Now, Aladdin had always kept his secret to himself. Only his mother knew it and she had never told a soul. Halima, alas, had been kept in the dark. And so, now, wanting to give Aladdin a surprise as well as make a good bargain, she fetched the old oil lamp she had seen Aladdin tuck away, and gave it to the merchant in exchange for a new one. The merchant quickly began to rub it . . . and the genie was now at the service of the wizard who had got his magic lamp back.

In a second he whisked away all Aladdin's possessions and magically sent the palace and the princess to an unknown land. Aladdin and the Sultan were at their wits' end. Nobody knew what had happened. Only Aladdin knew it had something to do with the magic lamp. But as he wept over the lost genie of the lamp, he remembered the genie of the ring from the wizard's finger.

Slipping the ring on his finger, Aladdin twisted it round and round.

"Take me to the place where the wizard has hidden my wife," he ordered the genie. In a flash, he found himself inside his own palace, and peeping from behind a curtain, he saw the wizard and the princess, now his servant.

"Psst! Psst!" hissed Aladdin.

"Aladdin! It's you . . .!"

"Ssh. Don't let him hear you. Take this powder and put it into his tea. Trust me." The powder quickly took effect and the wizard fell into a deep sleep. Aladdin hunted for the lamp high and low, but it was nowhere to be seen. But it had to be there. How, otherwise, had the wizard moved the palace? As Aladdin gazed at his sleeping enemy, he thought of peering underneath the pillow. "The lamp! At last," sighed Aladdin, hastily rubbing it.

"Welcome back, Master!" exclaimed the genie. "Why did you leave me at another's service for so long?"

"Welcome," replied Aladdin. "I'm glad to see you again. I've certainly missed you! It's just as well I have you by me again."

"At your command," smiled the genie.

"First, put this wicked wizard in chains and take him far away where he'll never be found again." The genie grinned with pleasure, nodded his head, and the wizard vanished. Halima clutched Aladdin in fear:

"What's going on? Who is that genie?"

"Don't worry, everything is all right," Aladdin reassured her, as he told his wife the whole story of how he had met the wizard and found the magic lamp that had enabled him to marry her. Everything went back to normal and the happy pair hugged each other tenderly.

"Can we return to our own kingdom?" the princess asked timidly, thinking of her father, so far away. Aladdin glanced at her with a smile.

"The magic that brought you here will

take you back, but with me at your side, forever."

The Sultan was almost ill with worry. His daughter had disappeared along with the palace, and then his son-in-law had vanished too. Nobody knew where they were, not even the wise men hastily called to the palace to divine what had happened. The jealous Chamberlain kept on repeating:

"I told you Aladdin's fortune couldn't last."

Everyone had lost all hope of ever seeing the missing pair again, when far away, Aladdin rubbed the magic lamp and said to the genie,

"Take my wife, myself and the palace back to our own land, as fast as you can."

"In a flash, Sire," replied the genie. At the snap of a finger, the palace rose into the air and sped over the Sultan's kingdom, above the heads of his astonished subjects. It gently floated down to earth and landed on its old site. Aladdin and Halima rushed to embrace the Sultan.

To this very day, in that distant country, you can still admire the traces of an ancient palace which folk call 'the palace that came from the skies.'

ALI BABA AND THE FORTY THIEVES

Once upon a time . . . in a distant Persian city lived two brothers called Ali Baba and Kasim. Ali Baba was terribly poor, and he lived with his wife in a mud hut. He picked up sticks in the woods and sold them in bundles at the market.

Kasim, however, had a rich wife, and he lived in a big fine house and sold carpets. He became richer than ever. One day, as Ali Baba was gathering sticks in a wood some way from the city, he heard a band of horsemen gallop towards him. Scared that he

might be in trouble for stealing wood, he scrambled up a tree and hid amongst the foliage, seconds before the men, armed to the teeth, rode underneath.

They were robbers, no doubt about that. Ali could tell by their evil looks, rough beards and bad language. But what made it perfectly clear to him was the booty they unloaded from their horses, obviously plundered in a raid. Their leader was a grim wicked-looking man. Followed by his men, he strode towards a rocky mountain nearby. Throwing wide his arms he suddenly shouted:

"Open sesame!"

Ali Baba could hardly believe his eyes. For at the robber's words, the rock face swung open to become the entrance to a deep, dark cave. The robbers trooped inside, dragging their sacks. Ali Baba was struck dumb by this amazing sight, and he crouched in his tree, without moving a muscle. He could hear the robbers' voices echo in the cave, then out they came. Again opening his arms, the leader exclaimed loudly:

"Close sesame!" And the rock swung tightly shut, as they leapt onto their horses and galloped away. Trembling with fear, Ali Baba climbed down the tree. He had just had the biggest shock of his life. Hardly aware of what he was doing, he muttered:

"Open sesame." But the mountain stood still. Ali Baba said the words again, but this time he shouted them. Suddenly, the rock began to move. Ali Baba lit a flare and entered the cave. In front of his bulging eyes lay vast piles of treasure: pots of silver and gold, precious vases, weapons studded with rubies and emeralds, diadems, carved plates and carpets, all heaped together.

The poverty-stricken stick-gatherer rubbed his eyes in disbelief. His hand was shaking like a leaf, as he picked up a gold coin.

"It's real!" he said in awe. Jabbering with excitement and stunned at the sight of such untold wealth, he told himself:

"I'll take some coins. Nobody will ever know!" And he filled four bags full. The second he reached home, Ali Baba locked the door and emptied the sacks in front of his astounded wife.

"Count them," he ordered her triumphantly, before telling her what had happened. But there were far too many coins for these poor people to count.

"We can't count them all. Run to my brother's house and ask him for a corn measure. We'll use that," said Ali Baba. When Kasim's wife heard this strange request, her curiosity was aroused.

"I wonder what they want to measure. It can't be corn, they're far too poor." And she quickly brushed a touch of tar across the bottom of the measuring pail. And when she got the pail back there was something stuck to it – as the clever woman had known there would be. It was a gold coin.

"A gold coin. Where did that come from? They're the poorest of the poor!" And she rushed off to tell her husband. Kasim was most annoyed.

"How dare my brother have gold coins without telling me about it," he snapped. And off he marched to ask Ali Baba for an explanation. Ali Baba innocently told Kasim his strange story, but asked him to keep it a secret. Of course, Kasim promised, but he quickly told his wife about it and ordered the servants to saddle ten sturdy mules for next morning.

"I'll be richer than ever. Incredibly rich!" he said to himself as he went to bed. But he didn't sleep a wink for thinking of the treasure. It was still dark when Kasim and his mule train set out. When he reached the mountain, beyond the forest, he pronounced the magic words and entered the cave. With a beating heart, he crammed as much as he could into the saddle bags. But Kasim's greed led to his downfall, for the bags were so stuffed with treasure that they became too heavy to lift. Kasim realised, with a sinking feeling, that he would have to leave behind some of his precious burden. But it took him a long time, and he was still picking over what to keep and what to abandon, when . . .

. . . as fate would have it, the robber band returned. When they saw that the entrance to the cave was open, they rushed inside with drawn swords. Unlucky Kasim was quickly discovered and killed. And the robbers were so fierce that they chopped him into four and left the pieces at the entrance.

"That will warn any other snooper of the end that awaits him!" shouted the leader.

Kasim's wife waited in vain for two days, then in desperation, she ran to Ali Baba and told him where her husband had gone, asking for help. Ali Baba was dismayed.

"He promised he would never . . ." However, Ali Baba was fond of his brother, so he saddled a mule and rode to the mountain. When he saw, to his horror, the remains of Kasim, he broke down and wept. Then he plucked up enough courage to wrap them in a rug, which he tied to the mule's back. But

Kasim's wife, when she saw what had happened to her husband, died of a broken heart. Ali Baba and his family went to live in Kasim's palace. There he met Morgantina, a clever young slave girl who had long been a servant in the palace. It was she who told Ali Baba that his brother's remains could be put together again before being buried. Mustapha, the cobbler, would do the job, for a good reward.

"I have to blindfold you," Morgantina told the cobbler, "so you can't see where you're going, then there won't be any gossip." The cobbler did his work well and was led, still blindfolded, back to his shop, with a bag of gold for his trouble.

In the meantime, when the robber leader saw that the body had been removed, he knew that someone else had found the treasure trove. Angry and alarmed, he ordered one of his men to sneak into the city and find out what he could. Well, by sheer chance, the spy had a hole in the sole of his boot and he went into the cobblers. Mustapha was bursting to tell someone all about his luck . . .

". . . and they gave me a bag of gold for stitching the body together again."

"If you take me to the place, I'll give you another bag of gold," said the robber immediately. The cobbler nearly danced for joy. Then his heart sank. How was he to find the house he had never seen?

"I'll blindfold you again," said the robber, "then you take your time and try to remember which way you went!" As it turned out, the robber was lucky, for Mustapha had an excellent sense of direction. What's more, he had counted his footsteps. So he counted them again:

". . . five hundred and ten, five hundred and eleven, five hundred and twelve. Here!" The cobbler wrenched the cloth from his eyes and found himself in front of Ali Baba's palace. The robber handed over the bag of gold and, unseen, drew a red cross on the door. Then he hurried away to give his leader the news.

Dusk fell and, as Morgantina was about to enter the palace, she noticed the strange mark. Her suspicions aroused, she quickly drew a red cross on all the other doors in the street. At dead of night the wicked band arrived to take revenge, but at the sight of all the red crosses, they stopped in their tracks. Which was the right door? Morgantina had unknowingly saved her master from death, and the leader of the gang put his man to the sword for giving him a false lead.

"You fools. Can't you do anything properly? I'll go to the city myself." Disguised as a merchant, he went to Mustapha. Delighted at the idea of earning more money, the cobbler took the robber to Ali Baba's palace. And the wicked man fixed in his mind the exact place and street. Back in his hideout, he ordered two of his men to buy a cart and thirty nine giant jars. Now, after the murder of the messenger, there were only thirty eight robbers left, and each one hid in a jar. The last jar was filled with oil, and loaded with the others onto the cart pulled by four horses. The robbers set off for the city. It was late when they reached the palace and Ali Baba himself came out.

"What can I do for you?" he said.

"I'm an oil merchant," replied the leader, "and I must be at market tomorrow. It's late and we're weary. Can you give us a bed for the night?" Pleased at being able to help, Ali Baba, who had known what it meant to be poor, warmly welcomed the merchant and his men and had the cart taken into the courtyard.

After a good meal, the leader of the band went back to the courtyard. He said he was going to make sure than none of the jars had been damaged during the journey, but in fact, he warned his men to be ready, at a signal, to leap from the jars and kill everyone in the palace. As the household slept, Morgantina lingered in the kitchen to tidy up. Suddenly, she thought she would have a sip of the merchant's oil to see if it was as tasty as her own. But when she lifted the lid from the first jar, to her horror, a gruff voice growled:

"Is it time?"

"No, not yet," muttered Morgantina hastily. At every jar, exactly the same thing happened, but the last one was filled with oil, which she dragged back into the kitchen. She then tipped the contents into a huge cauldron and heated it over the fire. Then, taking a jugful of boiling oil, Morgantina poured it over the head of a robber. She then poured the oil over every one of the robbers and, in this way, wiped out the whole band. Then she hid in a corner. A little later, the leader of the robber band hurried into the courtyard to give the signal to attack. But when he raised the lids, he found to his terror that every one of his men was dead. Horrified, he could not fathom what trap he had fallen into. The robber fled into the night.

Next morning, Morgantina told Ali Baba of her adventure.

"I'll never be able to thank you enough!" exclaimed Ali Baba. "You are an amazing girl. From this second you are no longer a slave, but a free member of this household."

The dead men were buried under cover of darkness, and Ali Baba was sure he had nothing more to fear. The leader of the robber band, however, had recovered from his shock and was eager for revenge. So he shaved off his beard, changed his looks and disguised himself as a carpet seller. At the market, he met Tabit, Ali Baba's son, who took a liking to him.

"Sooner or later this silly chap will invite me home," said the false carpet seller, "then I can murder them all."

"That merchant has sold you some fine carpets very cheaply," remarked Ali Baba to his son. "Ask him to come to the house." When Morgantina saw the guest, she felt sure his face was familiar. Then she remembered. The carpet seller and the leader of the band were one and the same person. Without saying a word, she went back to the kitchen, but later she asked Ali Baba if she might dance for the guest.

"If you like," said Ali Baba. When coffee was served, Morgantina entered in a swirl of veils to the beat of her tambourine. In her right hand she held a knife. As she stopped dancing, she thrust the knife into the carpet seller's heart.

"He's one of the robbers!" she cried. "I know his face. He would have killed us all." Morgantina had once more saved their lives! Tabit hugged her, little knowing that his joy would soon turn to love and that they would marry. Ali Baba was the only person left who knew the secret of the treasure. He made wise use of it for many years, but he never told anyone the magic words that would open the cave of the Forty Thieves.

123

THE PARROT SHAH

Once upon a time . . . hundreds of years ago, there lived a brave young Shah. His counsellor was a very old wise Minister called Saleb.

Like all his subjects, the Shah worshipped the God of Reason. Every day, he went to the temple he had built close to the palace. In response to the prayers, the God gave the Shah good advice on the difficult art of government. Indeed, the kingdom had never been so well ruled and had become very prosperous. One day, at the end of his first visit, the Shah was amazed to hear the God's deep voice say: "You no longer need my advice. You are wise enough. You can keep on praying to me, but this is the last time you will speak to me. But before I leave you to Fate, I will grant you a wish. Anything you ask will be given to you."

On his knees before the statue, the Shah thought for a long time before replying. Then he said: "Oh, God who rules over us all, thank you for all you have done for me and my people. Give me the power to transfer my soul into the body of another man or animal, whenever I want. And let my own body remain intact till I enter it again."

"It shall be so," said the God. "Now listen carefully . . ." Back at the palace, the Shah quickly called the Chief Minister.

"Would you believe it, Saleb! In his infinite goodness, the God has given me his trust and a great power . . ." and he told his counsellor all about it. The old man, however, had great doubts about the wisdom of this, but he hid his feelings.

"This strange incredible thing could change my master's whole life and destiny," the old man told himself. "I must do my best to make sure he doesn't alter his ways and makes no dangerous changes. What he needs is a wife and family to keep him from making risky decisions. It only takes strange deeds to ruin good government."

Far beyond the mountains bordering on the Shah's kingdom lay a great fertile plain, the realm of an old king, who had an only daughter named Gala. Gala was young and beautiful and so sweet and gentle that her father hated the thought of letting her get married. The Court, however, was eager to see her a bride. The king was very possessive and wanted to keep Gala all to himself, and with the help of a wizard, he had thought up a plan to discourage her suitors. A magic tree was planted in the garden, a huge pomegranate that had three fruits. At sunset, the branches bent over to touch the ground and the fruit split open. Inside each lay a soft feather bed. Gala, the princess, slept in the middle one, with her servants on each side. The fruit closed over the maidens and the branches swung back to the sky, carrying the princess high above all danger. Seven walls were built round the garden, each studded with thousands of spikes which nobody could ever cross. The king sent out a proclamation:

"Any man wishing to marry my daughter must be noble, rich and handsome. But he must also succeed in picking the fruit in which the princess sleeps. Yet, if he falters in trying to cross the seven circles of spikes, he will be left to die." As it so happens, the Shah's Chief Minister decided that the princess would make a

good wife for his master. As time went by, many fine brave warriors perished on the spikes guarding the enchanted garden. Saleb, however, was sure that the special divine powers of the Shah would help him to overcome any obstacle. So he wanted to persuade the Shah to try and win the princess's hand. Every day, Saleb described the trials men had to go through to reach the king's daughter, and to begin with, the Shah was amused by such stories. Then

he became curious and began to ask questions himself. The clever Minister told his master of the princess's beauty and all about her brave suitors. In the end, the Shah began to fall in love with the girl he had never seen, just by hearing so much about her. In no time at all, he began to pore over ways of reaching the fruit. And the Chief Minister was delighted to hear of the Shah's plans.

Next day, the Shah ordered a large, brightly feathered parrot with a strong beak to be brought to him. He had decided to use his own magic powers, and he said to Saleb:

"My soul is going to enter this parrot, but my lifeless body will lie here till my return. Watch over it day and night till I come back."

After a long prayer to the God of Reason, the Shah did everything he had been told and fell into a deep sleep. His breathing grew fainter and fainter till it died away and he lay still on the bed. Watching worriedly, Saleb saw that the parrot, which had been sitting quietly on its perch, was now flapping its wings wildly. The Chief Minister opened the window and the bird flew away.

The parrot quickly reached the mountain. The air was cold and he flapped heavily upwards, but the highest peak was soon left behind. Far below lay the turrets of the palace and the glinting of thousands of spikes. Somehow, the parrot struggled across the rows of sharp steel and landed safely beside the magic tree.

The sun was setting when Gala and her two servants stepped into the fruit for the night. As the pomegranates closed, the calls

of the three maidens rang in the ears of the Parrot Shah, and in
the second before they shut, he caught a fleeting glimpse of the
beautiful princess. Her gleaming dark eyes seemed to smile at
him. Then the branches rose into the air and the fruit shrank back
to their normal size. As they pointed upwards, the parrot sprang
into the air and, with a blow of his strong beak, ripped the
pomegranate containing the princess from its branch. Clutching
the fruit in his claws, he flew off into the night.

The twinkling stars lit the Parrot Shah's path home. This time it
was hard to cross the mountain, but the parrot felt neither cold
nor fatigue, for he could still picture Gala's lovely face. As he
gripped the magic pomegranate, the parrot knew that it was
hindering his flight, and his wings grew weary and slow. In panic,
he felt he was going to drop the fruit, but the thought of Gala's
eyes filled him with new strength. Suddenly he saw the valley.
He was over the mountain. Now, he had to find the energy to go
on and re-enter his own body. And then admire Gala, the bride
of his dreams.

Saleb had been watching at the window, left open day and night, and guarding his master's lifeless body. Full of remorse at having coaxed the Shah into undertaking such a dangerous mission, the poor Minister had never stopped praying. Suddenly, he leapt to his feet:

"Thank Heavens!" he cried. "At last! At last! . . " The stars were fading and the sun coming up, tinting the clouds with pink, when the parrot appeared. Gently laying its precious burden on the bed, the bird went back to its perch . . . and the Shah's body came slowly to life. Saleb threw himself in front of his master.

131

"Sire!" he gasped. "I've been so afraid. I thought I'd never see you again." The magic worked as the sun rose over the horizon and its first rays shone through the window. The pomegranate began to grow and grow as it did each morning, then it gently opened and out stepped Gala, smiling.

"Where am I? How did I get here?" she gasped in surprise. The Shah clasped her hand and kissed it fleetingly.

"You're in your future husband's palace!" The Chief Minister clapped his hands in delight. The wedding took place the very next day and the couple ruled happily ever after.

From that day, all the parrots in the Shah's kingdom were treated with great respect. A parrot was even included in the royal coat-of-arms and fluttered from the army's banners, while to all the people it was a sacred symbol.

THE WEEPING PRINCESS

Once upon a time . . . a greedy emperor forced his subjects to pay heavy taxes. Not only the poor were squeezed, but the nobles in this immense empire were highly taxed too. At last, tired of being crushed by taxes, the nobles held a protest meeting. When the emperor heard about this, he took fright for he feared a rebellion. So he sent out this proclamation to put an end to their complaints:

"The nobleman that can make my daughter Sarah smile again, for she's mourning the loss of her fiancé, will never pay taxes again."

This caused an uproar at the protest meeting. Most of the princes decided there was no need now to complain; for each was quite sure he would succeed where others might fail. So off they went to get ready to try and make Sarah smile. But some of the nobles warned their fellows that, with his words, the emperor was not really abolishing any taxes at all. From that day on, a long procession of noble knights trooped from all over the empire to the palace to try and console the weeping princess.

The crowds cheered them as they passed, but when they returned with bowed heads, the same crowds booed and whistled at their failure. The days went by and the list of defeated knights grew longer . . . Indians, Circassians, Arabs and Turks . . . from all over the provinces came bold young men, bouncing with confidence and hope. But the minute the princess set eyes on them, she just wept and wept. The emperor was delighted, for each failure meant another taxpayer. Even the common folk seemed contented to see that the rich too did not always get what they wanted. The only unhappy person among them was Sarah, who went on weeping.

135

One day, a Mongol prince seemed to be on the point of winning a smile. He thrummed his balalaika for hours, playing first a sad tune, then a more cheerful one, till he finished by playing a merry jig. The princess sat for ages staring at him dry-eyed and the onlookers thought she was about to smile. Instead she burst into floods of tears, to everyone's disappointment. A Kurdish chief, famed for his humour, who had already kept the court in fits of laughter, tried to steal a smile from Sarah with his witty remarks. But the princess's dark eyes filled with tears. Noblemen came from as far away as Persia, but in vain.

The only person who had not yet appeared was Omar, the chief of the tiniest farthest away province. A bright, intelligent young man, he had cleverly got the better of certain greedy ambitious relatives that tried to take away his power when he succeeded his uncle as chief. The emperor's messengers had taken a long time to reach this remote realm, and though Omar set out at once, on hearing the news, he rode for many days on his fine black horse. Then, one evening, he reached the palace. When the tired and dusty traveller explained to the stable boys why he had come, they laughed in scorn. But they had orders to obey, so they told him to enter.

"It's late," they said, "and you won't see the princess till tomorrow."

The emperor's other daughters, however, were soon told of the new arrival. "He's the most handsome of them all!" exclaimed one of the servants. So Marika, the emperor's youngest and prettiest daughter, with her sisters, peeked through a window at the sleeping Omar. Next morning, the emperor ordered the newcomer to be led before Sarah. The court crowded round to watch. Unlike all the other suitors, Omar did nothing at all to amuse the princess. He stared at Sarah without saying a word. And she stared back, with an empty look on her face. The two young people stared silently at each other. Then Omar went back to the emperor and said:

"Sire! Give me your sceptre and I will solve the problem of Sarah." Surprised at such an odd request, the emperor followed Omar into Sarah's room. The other princesses clustered round, smiling and admiring the handsome young man. With a deep bow to Sarah, Omar straightened up and dealt her a blow on the head with the sceptre. Screams filled the air: the emperor threw up his arms in rage and his daughters fled in all directions. The guards drew their swords. Then the whole room stopped in amazement. For, out of Sarah's head, which had been chopped off by the blow, rolled broken springs and pieces of metal. The princess that never smiled was a doll! A perfect doll! And nobody had ever been aware of it, except Omar.

The only princess that couldn't stop laughing was Marika. The emperor glared at her.

"Be quiet . . ." he ordered. But he too saw the funny side of it. For the crafty emperor had been making use of Sarah the doll as a way of guaranteeing himself a steady flow of taxes from all his subjects. And now, a man more cunning than himself had exposed his trick. The emperor had a sudden thought: he would rid himself of the cheeky Marika and gain an astute son-in-law able to help him hold onto his kingdom.

"You should be put to death for this insolence," he said, "but I'm going to spare your life, if you marry my youngest daughter. Of course, you won't need to pay taxes!" Smiling at a happy Marika, Omar nodded silently. Down in the depths of his mind he was thinking:

"One day, dear father-in-law, I'll be sitting on your Imperial throne." And he was, a few years later.

SASHA, MANSOR AND THE STORKS

Once upon a time . . . in Persia there lived a handsome young man called Sasha, who was the Ruler and greatly loved by all. Sasha had only one enemy, Kashenor, a cruel wicked wizard whose desire was to put his own son Mizrah on Sasha's throne.

Sasha loved to collect ancient precious objects, and he always granted an audience to any passing merchants. One day, Kashenor, disguised as a merchant, was taken by Mansor, the Chief Minister, before Sasha. The Ruler bought everything the merchant offered him, but he also asked what was inside a small drawer in an antique box.

"I really don't know myself," replied Kashenor, pulling out of the drawer an old roll of paper written in a long-forgotten language, together with a tobacco jar full of black powder.

"I'll give it to you as a present," he told the Ruler. Sasha wanted to know what the writing meant, so he gave the paper to his wise men, and a few days later, they told him what it said:

"The man that reads these words will acquire the power to turn

himself into an animal, any animal he likes, and to know its language. All he must do is to sniff the black powder and say the word MUTABOR. To turn back to a man again, he must bow three times to the east and repeat the word!"

But the roll of paper also contained a warning. It told the reader he must never laugh when in his animal shape, for he would then forget the magic word forever.

"Did you hear that, Mansor!" exclaimed the Ruler. "We can turn into animals! Shall we do it?"

"Sire, I'll do whatever you want me to," replied the Chief Minister with a low bow.

"Good! Then we'll try it tomorrow." At dawn next day, the Ruler and his Minister left the palace, and when they were well out of sight, Sasha took the tobacco jar from his pocket.

"What animal shall we choose?" he asked the Minister. Now Mansor had no idea, till he noticed a stork glide past.

"Storks!" he cried. "Let's become storks!"

Sasha sniffed the powder and together the two said the word MUTABOR. Suddenly, their legs shrivelled into long thin limbs and their clothes became snowy white feathers, covering their whole bodies. All trace of the Ruler and his Chief Minister simply vanished. The two storks gaped at each other in astonishment. They flapped their wings and discovered they knew how to fly. At first, they were awkward, but soon became quite good at it.

"Doesn't the ground look so different from the air? Let's go and find other storks," suggested Sasha cheerfully, so they headed towards a river estuary. What a lot of bird things they learned on the way. Sasha and Mansor found it so silly to see a stork prancing stiffly around in his funny dance that they forgot all about the warning and began to laugh. They were later to regret bitterly that laughter . . .

Full of their new knowledge, the two storks decided, as the afternoon wore on, to return to the palace. Slowly and majestically they flew over the city. Something had happened in their absence, for they could see that the streets were thronged with spectators and a long procession was entering the portals of the palace. Sasha was furious to see a stranger sitting in his golden carriage, escorted by his own servants and guards. Wicked Kashenor's trick had worked, for the wizard's son was on his way to seize the Ruler's throne.

"Hurry!" urged Sasha. "We must dash back to the palace. Who is that imposter?"

"It's the son of Kashenor, that wizard you once banned from the palace," replied Mansor in horror. "He swore he'd get even. Remember?"

But even as he spoke, the Chief Minister shook with fear, for what he himself could not remember was the magic word. The two storks landed on the ground, ready to become humans again, but Sasha could only stammer . . . "I don't remember . . . I don't remember . . ." They looked at each other sadly: "We'll never be human beings again!"

Followed by the Ruler, the Chief Minister rose into the air.

"We'll go to Mecca and pray on the Prophet's tomb. Perhaps he'll help us remember the magic word." But Mecca was a long way away and the sun was setting. Tired and hungry, the two storks landed amongst the ruins of an old temple. As they looked around them, seeking food and water, a sudden long-drawn out screech made them jump in fright. Who on earth was living in such a lonely place? Sasha plucked up courage.

"Let's go and find out!" he said, and off they went through the crumbled buildings. From a

dark corner, a pair of big yellow eyes glowed and the mournful cry of some strange creature echoed louder than before. It was a huge owl.

"Thank goodness," it said, "I've been waiting for years. The spell is sure now to be broken . . ." Sasha and Mansor stared at each other in amazement on hearing the owl talk.

"Who are you?" they asked it.

"I'm Naja, the King of India's daughter. Many years ago, an evil wizard called Kashenor wanted me to marry his son Mizrah, so that he could seize my father's kingdom. One day, disguised as a slave, Kashenor gave me a cool drink in the garden. That turned me into an owl. Kashenor said I'd remain a horrible bird till the day someone came, wanting to marry me. That's why I've been sentenced to making my home in these ruins."

"So you're one of Kashenor's victims too!" exclaimed the Ruler, and he went on to tell the owl his own story.

"What shall we do now?" they asked themselves.

"There's hope yet," replied the owl. "For now and again, Kashenor meets the other wizards in one of the ruined halls.

While they're banqueting, they boast of what they've done. If Kashenor should brag of what he did to you, then he might repeat the magic word you've forgotten!"

"Goodness, yes!" agreed the storks. "Let's go to the hall." But the owl sat where she was.

"Before we go," she said, "one of you must promise to marry me. Otherwise I'll remain a bird forever!"

"Very well! I promise I'll marry you, but only if I manage to hear the magic word and break the spell," said the Ruler.

So the owl led the storks along a narrow passage beneath the temple, to a hall.

"This is their meeting place. We can spy on them from this hole." The three

birds took turns at keeping watch. Then one evening, the murmur of voices announced the arrival of the wizards. As they ate and toasted each other's health, Kashenor rose to his feet.

"Guess how I succeeded in placing my son on the Ruler's throne?" he said, and when the wicked wizard said the word MUTABOR, the two storks thrilled with delight.

"Mutabor! Mutabor!" they repeated. "That's the magic word!"

Outside in the open air, the storks bowed three times to the east and said the magic word. Instantly they became men again, and the owl magically turned into a beautiful young lady. The three hugged each other with joy.

"I will keep my promise," he assured her, "and when I am on my throne, I shall marry you."

The Ruler's next task was to depose Mizrah. Stealing the wizards' camels, they rode all night, and dawn found them at the city gates.

"The Ruler is alive!" cried the first people to see them. As they rode through the streets, the citizens pressed round, cheering wildly.

"Sasha has come back! Mizrah has lied to us!" The wizard's nasty plan had failed. With a handful of followers, Mizrah had succeeded in seizing the throne, certain that Sasha would never be seen again. But when he heard the news, the wizard's son tried to escape. However, he was captured and thrown into prison. Kashenor too was put in chains, and the citizens themselves pronounced the sentence, when they learned what he and his son had done.

"Death! Put them to death!" shouted the Ruler's subjects. And so the wizard was executed. Mizrah, instead, was forced to sniff the black powder that had caused all the trouble and speak the magic word MUTABOR. He instantly turned into a stork and was sent to live in a cage at the top of the highest turret.

And in the end, this whole affair, brought much happiness to the palace, for Naja turned out to be the perfect wife of Sasha's dreams.

Once upon a time . . .

a miller died leaving the mill to his eldest son, his donkey to his second son and . . . a cat to his youngest son.

"Now that's some difference!" you might say; but there you are, that's how the miller was!

PUSS IN BOOTS

The eldest son kept the mill, the second son took the donkey and set off in search of his fortune . . . while the third sat down on a stone and sighed,

"A cat! What am I going to do with that?" But the cat heard his words and said,

"Don't worry, Master. What do you think?

That I'm worth less than a half-ruined mill or a mangy donkey? Give me a cloak, a hat with a feather in it, a bag and a pair of boots, and you will see what I can do." The young man, by no means surprised, for it was quite common for cats to talk in those days, gave the cat what he asked for, and as he strode away, confident and cheerful, the cat said, "Don't look so glum, Master. See you soon!"

Swift of foot as he was, the cat caught a fat wild rabbit, popped it into his bag, knocked at the castle gate, went before the King and, removing his hat, with a sweeping bow, he said:

"Sire, the famous Marquis of Carabas sends you this fine plump rabbit as a gift."

"Oh," said the King, "thanks so much."

"Till tomorrow," replied the cat as he went out. And the next day, back he came with some partridges tucked away in his bag. "Another gift from the brave Marquis of Carabas," he

announced. The Queen remarked,

"This Marquis of Carabas is indeed a very courteous gentleman."

In the days that followed, Puss in Boots regularly visited the castle, carrying rabbits, hares, partridges and skylarks, presenting them all to the King in the name of the Marquis of Carabas. Folk at the palace began to talk about this noble gentleman.

"He must be a great hunter," someone remarked. "He must be very loyal to the King," said someone else. And yet another, "But who is he? I've never heard of him." At this someone who wanted to show people how much he knew, replied,

"Oh, yes, I've heard his name before. In fact, I knew his father."

The Queen was very interested in this generous man who sent these gifts. "Is your master young and handsome?" she asked the cat.

"Oh yes. And very rich, too," answered Puss in Boots. "In fact, he would be very honoured if you and the King called to see him in his castle." When the cat returned home and told his master that the King and Queen were going to visit him, he was horrified.

"Whatever shall we do?" he cried. "As soon as they see me they will know how poor I am."

"Leave everything to me," replied Puss in Boots. "I have a plan." For several days, the crafty cat kept on taking gifts to the King and Queen, and one day he discovered that they were taking the Princess on a carriage ride that very afternoon.

153

The cat hurried home in great excitement. "Master, come along," he cried. "It is time to carry out my plan. You must go for a swim in the river."

"But I can't swim," replied the young man.

"That's all right," replied Puss in Boots. "Just trust me." So they went to the river and when the King's carriage appeared the cat pushed his master into the water.

"Help!" cried the cat. "The Marquis of Carabas is drowning." The King heard his cries and sent his escorts to the rescue. They arrived just in time to save the poor man, who really was drowning. The King, the Queen and the Princess fussed around and ordered new clothes to be brought for the Marquis of Carabas.

"Wouldn't you like to marry such a handsome man?" the Queen asked her daughter.

"Oh, yes," replied the Princess. However, the cat overheard one of the ministers remark that they must find out how rich he was.

"He is very rich indeed," said Puss in Boots. "He owns the castle and all this land. Come and see for yourself. I will meet you at the castle."

And with these words, the cat rushed off in the direction of the castle, shouting at the peasants working in the fields, "If anyone asks you who your master is, answer: the Marquis of Carabas.

Otherwise you will all be sorry." And so, when the King's carriage swept past, the peasants told the King that their master was the Marquis of Carabas.

In the meantime, Puss in Boots had arrived at the castle, the home of a huge, cruel ogre. Before knocking at the gate, the cat said to himself, "I must be very careful, or I'll never get out of here alive." When the door opened, Puss in Boots removed his feather hat, exclaiming, "My Lord Ogre, my respects!"

"What do you want, cat?" asked the ogre rudely.

"Sire, I've heard you possess great powers. That, for instance, you can change into a lion or an elephant."

"That's perfectly true," said the ogre, "and so what?"

"Well," said the cat, "I was talking to certain friends of mine who said that you can't turn into a tiny little creature, like a mouse."

"Oh, so that's what they say, is it?" exclaimed the ogre. The cat nodded,

"Well, Sire, that's my opinion too, because folk that can do big things never can manage little ones."

"Oh, yes? Well, just watch this!" retorted the ogre, turning into a mouse. In a flash, the cat leapt on the mouse and ate it whole. Then he dashed to the castle gate, just in time, for the King's carriage was drawing up. With a bow, Puss in Boots said,

"Sire, welcome to the castle of the Marquis of Carabas!" The King and Queen, the Princess and the miller's son who, dressed in his princely clothes, really did look like a marquis, got out of the carriage and the King spoke:

"My dear Marquis, you're a fine, handsome, young man, you have a great deal of land and a magnificent castle. Tell me, are you married?"

"No," the young man answered, "but I would like to find a wife." He looked at the Princess as he spoke. She in turn smiled at him.

To cut a long story short, the miller's son, now Marquis of Carabas, married the Princess and lived happily with her in the castle. And from time to time, the cat would wink and whisper, "You see, Master, I am worth a lot more than any mangy donkey or half-ruined mill, aren't I?"

TIL ULENSPIGHEL

Once upon a time there lived a little boy called Til Ulenspighel. His father was a good blacksmith, his mother a kindly woman, but they never imagined that they had brought into the world the naughtiest rascal ever heard of! Til had such a lively personality, bright and naughty, that people couldn't help smiling when they saw him. And he got up to such mischief and all sorts of tricks, that we can't help smiling to ourselves . . . But as you'll soon see, the ones who didn't see the funny side of things were his fellow citizens. The minute he learned to speak, Til pulled people's legs. If a man, for instance, had flat feet, Til would greet him by saying,

"Good day, Mr. Flatfeet!" And if a lady had a red nose, he would say, "Good evening, Mrs. Rednose!" He enjoyed playing tricks and teasing everyone. Of course, the neighbours complained to his father, saying,

"Mr. Ulenspighel, what a rude son you have!" And so, one day Til's father said to him,

"Listen, son, why don't people like you? Do you annoy them?"

"Who, me?" said Til with an innocent air. "I never bother anyone. It's other people that shake their fists at me whenever they see me and say nasty things."

"Hmm!" said his father. "I wonder if that's really so. I'm going to market with the donkey. Get up behind!" Till didn't need to be told twice and he clambered behind his father.

But the second he was on the donkey's back, he hung a notice on his shoulders on which he had written: 'Whoever reads this is a donkey.' People *did* read it and they were offended, so they shook their fists and shouted, "Oh, you horrid boy, Til! What a little horror you are!" On hearing these shouts, Til's father, who knew nothing about the notice, muttered:

"You're right, Til. People are angry with you, though goodness knows why! Don't worry," he added, "come and sit in front and we'll see if they still call you names." Til did as he was told and slung the notice over his chest. Though his father couldn't see it, he could see other people as they shook their fists, scowled, shouted and yelled insults, and he said, "Folk don't like you, Til. But pay no attention to them and go your own way!" And Til laughed up his sleeve. . . .

Time went by and Til began to weary of long faces every time people saw him. He joked and teased folk now and again, but what harm was there in that? All he wanted to do was amuse himself and others as well. One day, a company of wandering entertainers came to the town: actors, sword swallowers and acrobats. They made a great impression on the lad, who stared at them open-mouthed. While holding a pole in their hands, they kept their balance as they walked the tightrope across the road. How he would love to do the same. The people who now shook their fists at him would clap their hands. No sooner thought than done, the boy picked up a pole, stretched a rope between two trees in the wood and started to practise. Of course, it wasn't easy and he fell more than once. But in the end, he felt pretty secure and decided to hold a show. He went through the streets crying,

"Tomorrow, Til Ulenspighel, the acrobat, will walk the tightrope!" Filled with curiosity, everyone came to watch.

Til had stretched the rope between his balcony and a tree in the nearby wood: the rope lay above the river and the young

lad climbed on. The crowd that, at first had laughed and made a noise, grew quiet after a while, and were impressed:

"He's clever all right," someone said. "He's a real acrobat," said someone else. "We were wrong about him!"

At that moment, Til's mother, who knew nothing about her son's gymnastics, hearing the murmur of the crowd, went onto the balcony . . . and saw her son walking the rope suspended over empty space. Frightened, she shouted,

"Til, come down at once!" And seeing that the boy was not doing as he was told, she picked up the scissors and cut the rope. Til fell with a splash into the river. You can imagine the people! First they started to laugh, snigger and make fun of the poor lad as he struggled soaking from the water.

"Hey, acrobat! If that had been the ground instead of water, you'd have had a cracked head, wouldn't you?" they called, chuckling, and Til said to himself, "Laugh if you want to, he who laughs last laughs longest! . . ."

Some days later, Til announced he was going to repeat the show, this time not over the river but above the main road. Everyone rushed to watch, hoping to see him fall off and hurt himself. Before he ventured on to the rope, Til called out, "To make it more difficult for me, I'm going to carry a sack on my back. Every spectator will give me his left shoe. I'll put it in the sack and hand it back at the end of the show." Everyone did this. Til walked the tightrope until he reached the middle of the road, and from the heights he said, "Now I'm going to give you back your shoes. There they are!" and opening the sack, he emptied out the shoes.

You can picture the confusion that reigned then. Not only did the onlookers get hit on the head by shoes, but everyone hunted for his own shoe without managing to find it; he'd pick one up, but it belonged to somebody else, and he'd throw it down again, and start to look for another, argue, exchange insults . . . and Til, from a window on high looked down on the pandemonium and chuckling said,

"Ha! He who laughs last laughs longest! . . ."

THE PEASANT, THE SNAKE AND THE FOX

Once upon a time, a peasant on his way home heard a feeble voice calling "Help! Help!" He looked round, took a careful step or two then realised that the sound was coming from beneath a large boulder. He asked in amazement: "Who's that calling?" And a voice replied,

"It's me. The rock rolled down over my hole and I'm shut in. I can't get out, I'm going to die. Please help me. Move the boulder." The peasant then asked:

"But who are you?"

"I'm a poor snake," came the reply.

"A snake? But if I let you out you will bite me."

"No, no, I promise I won't. Get me out, please!" The peasant allowed himself to be persuaded and he shifted the boulder . . . and out of a hole in the ground slid a snake which darted towards the peasant and tried to bite him. The man jumped back and cried,

"Why did you do that?" The snake replied, "Because every good deed is rewarded by an evil one, didn't you know that?"

"No, I didn't. I don't think that's so," said the peasant.

"Very well," said the snake. "Let's go and ask someone. If we come across someone who thinks as you do, well, that's it, but if people say I'm right, then I shall bite you. Agreed?"

"Agreed," said the peasant, and off they went.

A little later, they met an old mangy lame horse, thin and covered in scratches, with an uncombed mane and dirty tail. The peasant spoke to him.

"Listen, friend. If someone does a good deed, what does he get as his reward?" Without a moment's hesitation, the horse replied.

"A bad deed. Look at me! I served my master faithfully for years and now that I'm old, he has left me to die of starvation!" At these words, the snake turned to the peasant and hissed, "Did you hear that? I shall bite you now!" But the man exclaimed: "Wait! One question isn't enough! We have to ask someone else."

"Bother!" exclaimed the snake. "Very well, let's look for someone else, but wait and see, I'm right and I'll get my bite!" So, leaving the horse behind, the pair went on their way.

They met a sheep which, at the peasant's question, said: "A good deed is always repaid with a bad deed. Look at me, I always follow my master and never complain. I obey him all the time and what does he do? He shears my fleece in winter, so I feel the cold, and makes me keep it in summer, so I melt with the heat!"

"Get ready," said the snake, "I'm about to bite!" But the peasant said,

"Please! We've had the first round, and the second one as well, now let's play the deciding round. If I'm wrong at the third question, then I'll let you bite me."

On they went, and in the wood, the peasant caught sight of a fox. Suddenly he had an idea. With an excuse, he left the snake on the road and ran into the wood to speak to the fox.

"Listen, fox, do you too think that a good deed is always rewarded by a bad one?"

"Of course!" replied the fox. Then the man went on.

"Well, listen, I'm going to ask you the same question in front of a snake. If you say that one good deed is rewarded by another good deed, I'll give you a present of a piglet, a lamb or a goose. How's that?"

"Good," said the fox. The peasant went back to the snake.

"I saw a fox over there," he said. "As you know, foxes are wise. Let's go and hear what he thinks about it." A little later they asked the fox the same question and the fox replied as had been agreed.

"A good deed is always rewarded with another good deed, but," he went on, "why ask me that question?"

"Because this snake, that I helped to escape from his hole blocked by a boulder, wants to bite me," replied the peasant. The fox looked at the snake and said, "Hmm! I think a snake can manage to slither under a boulder."

"But it was a big boulder," the snake protested, "and it was blocking the entrance to my den."

"I don't believe you!"

"Oh, don't you? Well come and see then," said the snake, setting off for his den with the fox and the peasant. Pointing to the boulder, he said, "See? That boulder fell just there," and he pointed to the entrance.

167

But the fox shook his head. "A big snake like you couldn't get into such a little hole," he said. Annoyed, the snake retorted,

"Don't you think so?" and slid swiftly into the hole. Then the fox shouted,

"Quick, peasant man! Shut him in!" and the peasant rolled the boulder back across the mouth of the den, imprisoning the snake (and I think he's in there yet!).

"Ah, fox," said the peasant happily, "now that was a good deed! You got rid of that wicked snake for me! Thanks a million!"

"Oh, it was nothing," replied the fox, "but don't forget that piglet, the lamb and the goose you promised me."

"No, I won't. Come to the farm this evening and you shall have them," said the man.

That same evening, the fox went to the farm, but the peasant appeared with two snarling dogs and a gun, shouting, "Get out of here, you horrible beast, if you don't want to get into trouble!"

The fox trotted away, sad and disappointed, muttering, "and they say I'm cunning! The cunning one is that peasant. Oh, well, that poor snake was probably right, good deeds are repaid with bad deeds," and off he went, his tail between his legs, into the wood.

THE WITCH IN THE TOWER

Once upon a time people in the Japanese city of Kyoto were terribly afraid; they shook with fear. A fierce witch had taken possession of the tower over the city gate which she opened and closed whenever she felt like it. She was capable of locking the gate in the face of travellers bringing food and merchandise, or throwing it wide open to savage tribes from the north. Many brave Samurai, the strongest and best fighters, had faced up to the witch, but the minute she set eyes on them, she hurled herself out of the tower, hair flying in the wind, screeching furiously and brandishing a fiery sword. Attacking them one by one, she left them lying dead in the dust. No, there was no hope for the city of Kyoto, and many people began to think of leaving it. The folk were murmuring,

"All our Samurai are dead. If only Watanabi were still here, the bravest of them all! But all that remains is his sword, and there's no one able to use it."

170

However, the sword was not all that remained of valiant Watanabi, there was also his son, a young boy. On hearing what the citizens were saying, he wondered,

"My father has gone, he died fighting, but we still have his sword. I shall take it and face the witch. Win or die, I shall be a credit to my father's memory." So the boy bravely armed himself and went off to the tower. The witch saw him arrive and she grinned, but did not make a move. She wouldn't even bother using her fiery sword on that snivelling youngster, she would wither him with a glance. So she paid little heed to Watanabi's son as he quietly crept into the tower, climbed the stairs without making the slightest sound and entered the witch's room. When, however, the witch heard the door close, she turned round and laid her wild burning gaze on the boy . . . but the splendour of Watanabi's sword blinded her.

"This is Watanabi's sword!" shouted the young boy, and before the witch could defend herself, he struck a blow and ended her life. In his father's memory and in honour of his sword, the boy had freed the city of Kyoto.

THE SEVEN OLD SAMURAI

Once upon a time, in far off Japan, a band of fierce robbers had their hiding place on top of a mountain almost always covered with grey clouds, windswept and battered by storms. The robbers lived in a large cave where they had piled their spoils. Now and again, they went down the mountain, attacked a village, murdered the poor folk they chanced upon, stole whatever they could lay hands on and burned it to the ground. Wherever the robbers

passed, there was nothing but smoking ruins, weeping men and women, misery, mourning and desolation.

The Emperor, worried at this, had sent his soldiers to attack the mountain, but the robbers had always managed to drive them off. The Emperor sent for one of the last remaining Samurai, old Raiko, and said to him:

"Raiko, you've served me for many years. Do my bidding for one last time. Go to the mountain at the head of an army and wipe out these bloodthirsty bandits." Raiko sighed.

"Your Majesty, if I were young again I'd do it alone. Today I'm too old, far too old to do that, or to command an army."

"Must I then," said the Emperor, "submit to the force of these marauding robbers?" The old Samurai replied:

"No, I'll go up there with six Samurai like myself."

"But if they're all as old as you, how can they help you?"

"Have faith in us!" said Raiko.

A few days later, the seven Samurai set off on their journey, not with horses, swords, shields and armour, which they could no longer have worn anyway, but dressed as humble pilgrims. From the summit, the bandits watched them come, and their leader said,

"Who cares about seven beggars. Let them climb up." The seven reached the cave and Raiko humbly said,

"Let us come in, it's cold outside. There's a wind blowing and we, as you can see, are old men. We'll be no trouble to you." The leader of the gang scornfully replied:

"Come in, old men, and stay in a corner." And so the seven pilgrims huddled in a corner while the bandits ate their meal of food stolen from the villages nearby.

Now and again, they threw scraps of food and leftovers to the old men, saying: "Eat this, and it is much too good for you." A few hours later, Raiko rose to his feet saying:

"The wind has dropped. We can go on our way. In thanks for your hospitality, we would like to offer you this liqueur, it is saké, rice wine. Drink our health with it." The robbers needed no second telling. In the blink of an eye, they had emptied the goatskin bottle Raika held out to them. And in the blink of an eye they all lay dead, for the saké contained a very potent poison. And so, the seven Samurai, too old to wield a sword, served the Emperor for the last time.

THE UNLUCKY WARRIOR

Once upon a time there was a Samurai called Hido. Valiant and strong, he was afraid of no-one, yet in all the wars he had ever fought, he had always found himself on the losing side. People in his home town began to say "Hido brings bad luck." And because nobody wanted him to fight for them any more the Samurai ended up a poor man. He said to himself:

"I'll go to a town where no-one knows me. Maybe I'll find work there." He gathered up his remaining belongings, his sword, bow and three arrows, and set off along the first road he came to. On and on he walked, until after many days march, he reached the banks of a lake. As he started to cross the narrow bridge over the water, he stopped in surprise. The way was blocked by an enormous snake, fast asleep. From its mouth and nostrils, it breathed red smoke with a pungent smell of sulphur. Hido thought to himself,

"That beast isn't going to stop *me*," and on tiptoe he stepped over the snake, without wakening it up, and went on his way. But he had barely gone twenty metres when he heard a voice behind him.

"Hey, you! Samurai!" He turned round. The snake had disappeared and in its place stood a well-dressed man, who made a friendly gesture and said,

"You're a brave one! You weren't scared of the snake. You see, I'm looking for a Samurai, and so, whenever I see someone coming, I turn into a snake. So far, you're the only person that has had the courage to step over it. What's your name?"

"Hido," replied the Samurai, "and who are *you*?" The man pointed to the lake.

"I'm King of that realm."

"What!" exclaimed Hido. "Is your realm a lake?" The King replied smiling,

"Yes. But under the water lies a great city protected by a crystal ball. My people live there happily, or at least they were happy until the Dragon arrived."

"The Dragon?" asked Hido. And the King replied sadly,

"Yes. Every second night, he dives off the bridge into the water, enters the crystal ball and creates havoc amongst my subjects. It won't be long before he eats us all. That's why I'm looking for a Samurai!"

Hido understood what he meant. "Do you want me to fight the Dragon?" he asked.

"Yes!"

"I think you ought to know, Sire, that people say I bring bad luck." To which the King replied:

"I never believe what I hear, only what I see. Come with me." He took Hido's hand and they went down into the lake. Wonder of wonders! The waters opened up and they went down to the great crystal circle that contained the city. There, Hido sat down with the King who gave him food and drink. Then he said, "In a little while you will hear a terrible noise. It will be the Dragon. You will have to face him up there, Hido."

"I'm not afraid. I have my sword, bow and three arrows."

"Only *three*? You will need a hundred arrows!" exclaimed the King. But Hido shook his head.

"They're poisoned, but even if they weren't, they would still be enough, because if the Dragon doesn't stop with three arrows in him, I wouldn't have time to fire any more." Just then there was a fearful noise and the sound of shouting.

"The Dragon! The Dragon!" Hido picked up his weapons and ran onto the bridge, only just in time. For the Dragon, huge and terrible, was advancing, with a roar, and breathing fire. Hido fired his first and second arrows, both of them hit the Dragon right in the heart, but it didn't stop.

Just as the Dragon was bearing down ferociously on him, Hido rememberd hearing that the only poison to stop a dragon is a man's saliva. So he licked his fingers and wet the tip of his last arrow, fired and hit the Dragon . . . On it came, still roaring. "All is lost," said Hido to himself . . .

. . . but after taking another step or two, the Dragon stopped in its tracks, shuddered and fell to the ground. It was dead. All the citizens rushed from the lake to greet Hido and shower him with gifts, telling him:

"Oh, brave Samurai, luck is with you and with our people!" So Hido knew that not only had he defeated the Dragon, he had overcome his bad luck.

THE RED DRAGON

Once there was a time, thousands of years ago, when animals were not the same as they are now. Except for a few like the lion, the tiger and the butterflies, they all looked alike. All were more or less the same height, everyone had four legs and it wasn't easy to tell which was which, even though the elephant did weigh more than the hyena, and the hippo more than the gazelle. One day, while all the animals were relaxing in a field, along came a red dragon, out of breath, crying,

"We're in danger, folks! The world is about to come to an end!"

"How do you know?" everyone asked. The dragon replied,

"I read it in the stars. We must escape!"

"But where can we go?" they asked him.

"To another world," he replied. "I'll take you there. I can fly and I'll take you to a planet that is safer than this one." Frightened, as they were, all the animals climbed on to the dragon's back.

With a bored look, the lion said, "I'm not scared of anything, so I'll just stay here on Earth." The others, however, were fighting to get on the dragon's back.

"Don't push, you behind!" shouted the crocodile.

"Hey, move that paw!" It was just like people today pushing and shoving to get onto an overcrowded train. At last the dragon cried,

"Ready! Off we go," and started to run for takeoff. The first and the second runs weren't fast enough, but at the third try he finally got off the ground, flapping his wings and waving his tail.

"Not so fast!" shouted somebody, and another voice yelled: "Faster, or we will end up in the trees!" The dragon replied,

"Oh, bother! I'm doing the best I can. Why don't you lot keep still, for once." The fact was that because they were frightened, they did everything but keep still, and so, after a while, the poor red dragon, now very tired, simply could not flap his wings any longer . . . and crashed on a lovely green meadow.

All the animals shrieked with terror. Nobody lost his life . . . but the snake lost his legs and slithered away through the grass. The rhino bumped his head and grew a horn. All the elephant's teeth fell out, except for two which became very long. The giraffe sprained his neck and it grew to a great length. The hippo rolled about so much he became nearly round, ended up in a pond and didn't come out, he was too ashamed to be seen . . . Well, in that fall, all the animals took on a different appearance and became what they are today. And when the lion saw them, what he said was:

"Oh, how funny you look!"

DOPEY DENNIS

Once upon a time, there was a little boy called Dennis. Everyone called him Dopey because . . . well, read on and you will see why. Dennis lived with his mother in a nice house with a courtyard, vegetable plot, cellar and a henrun. One day his mother, since she had to go shopping, said to him,

"I'll be away for an hour or two, son. Now, the broody hen is sitting on her eggs. Make sure nobody goes near her. Keep the house tidy and don't touch the jar in the cupboard, it's full of poison."

"Don't worry, Mum," the little boy said, and when his mother had gone, he went into the yard to keep guard over the broody hen. However, tired of sitting, the hen got up to stretch her legs for a little before going back to the eggs. Dennis picked up a stick and yelled:

"You nasty creature, get right back on those eggs!"

But the broody hen, annoyed, only said, "Cluck!", and so
Dennis hit her with his stick. He didn't really mean to do her
any harm, but the blow fell on the middle of her neck and the
poor hen dropped dead.

"Oh!" gasped the lad. "Who's going to sit on the eggs now?
Well, I had better do something about that!" So he sat on the
eggs . . . and broke the lot! Getting up with the seat of his
trousers sticky with egg yolk, Dennis said to himself, "Mum will
give me such a scolding. But to keep in her good books, I'll
give her a surprise, I'll make the lunch." He picked up the hen,
plucked its feathers and put it on the spit to roast.

"A roast calls for a good wine!" he said to himself. He took a
jug and went down to the cellar where he started to draw
sparkling red wine from a barrel. "Mum will be pleased with
me," he told himself. At that moment, there was a dreadful
noise in the kitchen. Dennis said to himself, "Who can that be? I
must go and see." And he went . . . forgetting to turn off the tap
on the barrel.

Up he ran to the kitchen and saw the cat with the roast hen in its jaws and the spit overturned. "Hey thief!" shouted the lad. "Put my hen down!" He picked up a rolling pin and started to chase the cat which, terrified as it was, firmly held on to the roast chicken as it dashed from room to room. The pair of them knocked against the cupboards, overturned tables, sideboards and stools, smashed vases, pots, plates and glasses. The devastation ended when the cat dropped the hen, leapt out of a window and vanished from sight. Dennis picked up his roast, laid it on the table and said:

"Now, I'll go and fetch the wine." He went back to the cellar . . . which was flooded with the wine that had poured out of the barrel. "Good gracious!" gasped Dennis. "What am I to do now?" He didn't dare go in, for before him streched a lake of red wine.

"I'll have to mop it all up," muttered Dennis to himself, "but how? I could go into the yard and get some sacks of sand, bring them into the cellar and scatter the sand over the floor . . . But that's much too hard work. I'd better think of something else, now then . . ." Seated on the bottom step, his elbows on his knees, holding his head in his hands, the lad tried to think of a good idea. It really was an alarming situation: there were nearly six inches of wine all over the floor and in it floated corks, bottles and bits of wood . . .

"I've got it!" Dennis suddenly exclaimed. He picked up one of the bags lying on a table, opened it . . . and started to scatter all the flour it contained. "Splendid! The flour will absorb the wine and I can walk about the cellar without wetting my feet," he cried.

In no time at all, he had spread not one but five bags of good flour on the floor. In the end, the floor was covered with a wine-coloured, soft, sticky paste, and as he walked on it, it stuck to his shoes. Dennis went to get the jug he had filled and carried it in great delight back to the table, leaving red footprints everywhere.

"Mum is going to be really pleased," he said.

Nevertheless, when he thought of all the mess he had made, he began to fear a scolding and maybe punishment too. "Never mind," he said, "I'll drink the poison and die." So he went to the cupboard and picked up the jar. He thought the poison would be a black liquid, but the jar contained a red cream. He picked up a spoon and said, "I'll eat it then instead of drinking it."

Just as he was about to take his first spoonful, he realised how silly he was. Nobody should ever eat poison, not even when your name is Dopey Dennis. Instead, he decided to hide from his mother so that she would not be able to punish him.

A quarter of an hour later, his mother returned. When she saw the overturned furniture, the broken plates and the red footprints, she got a fright and cried, "Dennis! What has happened? Where are you? Answer me!"

There was no reply, but she suddenly noticed a pair of legs sticking out of the oven.

"I'm not surprised you are hiding from me, Dennis, after causing all this mess," she said. "Well, while I am clearing up after you, you can take this roll of cloth to the market and try and sell it for a good price." And she handed the boy a roll of cloth as she spoke. "Oh, I will," said Dennis. "Leave it to me."

When he got to market, Dennis began to shout, "Cloth! Who'll buy this lovely cloth?" Several women came over and asked him,

"What kind of cloth is it? Is it soft? Is it hard-wearing? Is it dear? How long is it? How much does it cost"? Dennis exclaimed:

"You talk too much, and I don't sell things to chatterboxes," and off he went. He passed by a statue and mistook it for a fine gentleman, so he asked it, "Sir, would you like to buy this fine cloth? Yes or no? If you don't say anything, that means you do. Look here! Do you like it? Yes? Good! Then take it," and he left the cloth beside the statue and went home.

"Mum! Mum!" he cried. "I've sold the cloth to a very well-dressed gentleman!" The woman asked:

"How much did he give you for it?" Dennis muttered,

"Oh! I forgot to ask him for the money! Don't worry, I'll go and ask him for it." He ran back to the statue but the cloth had gone. Someone had clearly taken it away. Said Dennis to the statue, "I see you've taken the cloth home already. Fine, now give me the money!" Of course, the statue did not reply. Dennis repeated his request, then losing his temper, he picked up a stick and began to beat the statue about the head . . . which broke off and rolled to the ground. Out of the head poured a handful of gold coins, hidden there by goodness knows who! Dennis picked up the coins, put the head back in position and went home.

"Look!" he called. And his mother stared in astonishment at this small fortune.

"Who gave you such a good price?" his mother asked him. The lad replied:

"A very dignified-looking gentleman. He didn't speak, and do you know where he kept his money? In his head!" At this, Dennis's mother exclaimed:

"Dennis, listen! You killed the broody hen, broke the eggs, flooded the cellar with wine, wasted five bags of flour, smashed plates, bottles, vases and glasses; you nearly ate the cream, if you think you're going to pull my leg as well, you're badly mistaken! Get out of here!" And grabbing the broom, she chased him out of the house.

"I don't want to see you again till tonight. Off you go into the vegetable plot." But, as the boy was sitting on the doorstep and did not budge, his exasperated mother picked up the first thing that came within her grasp and hurled it at Dennis's head. It was a big basket of dried figs and sultanas. Dennis shouted then:

"Mum! Mum! Quick! Bring a bag! It's raining dry figs and sultanas!" His mother slumped into a chair and said sorrowfully:

"What can I do with a boy like him?"

Now, since Dennis went about telling folk he had a lot of gold coins, the magistrates sent for him. "Where did you find those coins?" they asked him. Dennis replied:

"A gentleman gave me them in payment for a roll of cloth."

"What gentleman?" said the magistrates severely.

"The gentleman that is always standing at the corner of Plane Tree Street and Jasmine Road," replied the boy.

"But that's a statue!" gasped the magistrates. Dennis said:

"He didn't say what his name was, but maybe it is Mr. Statue. He kept his money in his head." The magistrates gaped at each other in utter astonishment. Then the chief magistrate asked:

"Tell us, Dennis, when did you do this piece of business?"

"It was the day it rained dry figs and sultanas!" the boy replied. Again the magistrates exchanged looks, and now certain that Dennis really was dopey, they said:

"You can go home, lad, you're free!"

And so Dennis went home and lived there happily with his mother. A bit dopey, yes, but he never did anybody any harm, and that's all that counts.

THE SLEEPING PRINCESS

Once upon a time there was a Queen who had a beautiful baby daughter. She asked all the fairies in the kingdom to the christening, but unfortunately forgot to invite one of them, who was a bit of a witch as well. She came anyway, but as she passed the baby's cradle, she said:

"When you are sixteen, you will injure yourself with a spindle and die!"

"Oh, no!" screamed the Queen in horror. A good fairy quickly chanted a magic spell to change the curse. When she hurt herself, the girl would fall into a very deep sleep instead of dying.

The years went by, the little Princess grew and became the most beautiful girl in the whole kingdom. Her mother was always very careful to keep her away from spindles, but the Princess, on her sixteenth birthday, as she wandered through the castle, came into a room where an old servant was spinning.

"What are you doing?" she asked the servant.

"I'm spinning. Haven't you seen a spindle before?"

"No. Let me see it!" The servant handed the girl the spindle . . . and she pricked herself with it and, with a sigh, dropped to the floor.

The terrified old woman hurried to tell the Queen. Beside herself with anguish, the Queen did her best to awaken her daughter but in vain. The court doctors and wizards were called, but there was nothing they could do. The girl could not be wakened from her deep sleep. The good fairy who managed to avoid the worst of the curse came too, and the Queen said to her,

"When will my daughter waken?"

"I don't know," the fairy admitted sadly.

"In a year's time, ten years or twenty?" the Queen went on.

"Maybe in a hundred years' time. Who knows?" said the fairy.

"Oh! What would make her waken?" asked the Queen weeping.

"Love," replied the fairy. "If a man of pure heart were to fall in love with her, that would bring her back to life!"

"How can a man fall in love with a sleeping girl?" sobbed the Queen, and so heart-broken was she that, a few days later, she died. The sleeping Princess was taken to her room and laid on the bed surrounded by garlands of flowers. She was so beautiful, with a sweet face, not like those of the dead, but pink like

those who are sleeping peacefully. The good fairy said to herself,

"When she wakens, who is she going to see around her? Strange faces and people she doesn't know? I can never let that happen. It would be too painful for this unfortunate girl."

So the fairy cast a spell; and everyone that lived in the castle – soldiers, ministers, guards, servants, ladies, pages, cooks, maids and knights – all fell into a deep sleep, wherever they were at that very moment.

"Now," thought the fairy, "when the Princess wakes up, they too will awaken, and life will go on from there." And she left the castle, now wrapped in silence. Not a sound was to be heard, nothing moved except for the clocks, but when they too ran down, they stopped, and time stopped with them. Not even the faintest rustle was to be heard, only the wind whistling round the turrets, not a single voice, only the cry of birds.

The years sped past. In the castle grounds, the trees grew tall. The bushes became thick and straggling, the grass invaded the courtyards and the creepers spread up the walls. In a hundred years, a dense forest grew up.

Now, it so happened that a Prince arrived in these parts. He was the son of a king in a country close by. Young, handsome and melancholy, he sought in solitude everything he could not find in the company of other men: serenity, sincerity and purity. Wandering on his trusty steed he arrived, one day, at the dark forest. Being adventurous, he decided to explore it. He made his way through slowly and with a struggle, for the trees and bushes grew in a thick tangle. A few hours later, now losing heart, he was about to turn his horse and go back when he thought he could see something through the trees . . . He pushed back the branches . . . Wonder of wonders! There in front of him stood a castle with high towers. The young man stood stock still in amazement,

"I wonder who this castle belongs to?" he thought.

The young Prince rode on towards the castle. The drawbridge was down and, holding his horse by the reins, he crossed over it. Immediately he saw the inhabitants draped all over the steps, the halls and courtyards, and said to himself, "Good heavens! They're dead!" But in a moment, he realised that they were sound asleep. "Wake up! Wake up!" he shouted, but nobody moved. Still thoroughly astonished, he went into the castle and again discovered more people, lying fast asleep on the floor. As though led by a hand in the complete silence, the Prince finally reached the room where the beautiful Princess lay fast asleep. For a long time he stood gazing at her face, so full of serenity, so peaceful, lovely and pure, and he felt spring to his heart that love he had always been searching for and never found. Overcome by emotion, he went close, lifted the girl's little white hand and gently kissed it . . .

At that kiss, the Princess quickly opened her eyes, and wakening from her long long sleep, seeing the Prince beside her, murmured:

"Oh, you have come at last! I was waiting for you in my dream. I've waited so long!"

Just then, the spell was broken. The Princess rose to her feet, holding out her hand to the Prince. And the whole castle woke up too. Everybody rose to their feet and they all stared round in amazement, wondering what had happened. When they finally realised, they rushed to the Princess, more beautiful and happier then ever.

A few days later, the castle that only a short time before had lain in silence, now rang with the sound of singing, music and happy laughter at the great party given in honour of the Prince and Princess, who were getting married. They lived happily ever after, as they always do in fairy tales, not quite so often, however, in real life.

Once upon a time . . .

. . . in the Far East there lived a sailor whose name was Sinbad. Nobody had ever escaped certain death as often as he had.

THE SEVEN VOYAGES OF SINBAD THE SAILOR

Once upon a time years and years ago in Baghdad there lived a porter called Sinbad. As he was passing a palace one day, he saw a bench in the great doorway and thought he would rest on it. So he put down his load, and was about to sit down when curiosity got the better of him and, slipping through the entrance, he went into the gardens. To Sinbad it was like heaven.

Everywhere there were flower beds, gushing fountains and palm trees, in whose shade many gentlemen were strolling, while pages served them with cakes and

drinks. Sinbad couldn't help exclaiming aloud:

"Well I never! Here I am, worked to the bone, poor and always hungry while other lucky men never carry burdens, but enjoy good food and drink. And yet, we're all Allah's sons! What a world of difference between me and the people who live here." Sinbad had barely stopped speaking when one of the pages came across to him and said:

"Come with me. My master wishes to speak to you." Rather alarmed, Sinbad followed the lad into a hall where the owner of the house was seated amongst his guests.

"Come in," he said. "What's your name?"

"Sinbad, the Porter."

"My name is Sinbad too. Sinbad the Sailor. I hear you've been complaining, but I'd like you to know that I became rich only by working hard and taking dreadful risks. All this during seven amazing but adventurous voyages. I haven't had an easy life, you know. Sit down and I'll tell you my story."

"My father," began Sinbad the Sailor, "was a merchant. When he died, he left me a fortune. I was young then and foolish, and I started to squander my riches until one day, I discovered my money

had gone. I didn't lose heart, however, for I decided to become a merchant like my father. With the money I earned from selling my furniture and carpets I bought all the goods I could and set out. I boarded a ship at Bassora with other traders and began to trade in every port. One day, the captain dropped anchor near a beautiful island and we went ashore. We had hardly lit the fires to cook our meal when the captain suddenly shouted;

'Quick! Get away! This is no island. It's a huge fish that's been sleeping on the waves so long that trees have grown on it. The heat from the fires is wakening it. It will dive to the deep any minute now. Back to the ship! Drop everything!'

Many managed to climb aboard again, but I was too far away and ended up in the sea. Luckily I found a floating empty barrel. Clinging to this and drifting with the winds and currents, I reached an island. As I came ashore, I saw a mare tethered to a stump. Then a man appeared and asked me:

'Who are you? Where have you come from?'

'I've been shipwrecked,' I said. The man went on:

'Follow me,' he said and took me to a cave, where he offered me some food. I told him of my adventure and he listened in amazement. I was dying to know why he kept his horse tethered at the shore.

'I used to be one of King Mihragian's grooms' he replied. 'When the moon is full, we tether the mares on the beach so they can meet with the sea horses. The foals that are born are so beautiful there are none like them in the whole world. This is the time of the new moon and the sea stallions arrive. When it's all over, I'll take you to the king. You're very lucky, you know, for you'd have died of hunger on this desert island if you hadn't met me.'

My rescuer introduced me to his friends and they gave me a friendly welcome. Later, back in the city, the grooms told the king about my adventure.

'It was Allah's will that you should be saved,' the ruler told me after listening carefully. 'It's your destiny to live a long life.' Because he felt I was under the protection of Allah himself, he showered me with gifts and favours. I was appointed harbourmaster; it was my job to keep a register of all freight in transit and so I found myself in an excellent post.

Just the same, I felt homesick, and every time a ship came in, I asked the captain if he was bound for Baghdad, for I intended to ask him for a passage home. One day, however, as I took a note of the cargo on a ship that had just tied up, I asked:

'Anything else on board?'

'Yes,' replied the captain. 'There's still a certain quantity of goods aboard. The owner was lost at sea and must have drowned. I'm going to see if I can sell them and take the money back to his family in Baghdad.'

'What was the name of the man who was lost?' I enquired.

'Sinbad the Sailor.' I let out a shout.

'I am Sinbad the Sailor! I clung to a barrel that saved my life and drifted ashore on an island. There, thanks be to Allah, I met the royal grooms. And it was the king himself who made me harbourmaster. The goods you're carrying on board your ship belong to me.'

'Well, what a story! I've never heard anything like it!' exclaimed the captain. 'Isn't there an honest soul left in the world?'

'Captain!' I gasped. 'Why won't you believe what I say?'

'Because it's perfectly obvious,' he replied, 'that you heard the trader had drowned and now, by inventing a ridiculous adventure, you hope to lay hands on his property!' At that point, I described to the captain every single thing that had taken place on board his ship since the moment it had weighed anchor. He was forced to believe I was telling the truth.

'Good gracious!' everyone gasped. 'We certainly never dreamt that you were safe and sound.'

I got my trading goods back and immediately thought of something precious to give to the king. He was astounded at what had happened, but everyone assured him that every word was true. He too gave me a gift and allowed me to leave with all my belongings. I went aboard. Some days later, I was at Bassora and then back to Baghdad. I had grown far richer than before and quickly forgot all my past suffering."

When Sinbad the Sailor had ended his tale, he gave Sinbad the Porter three gold coins and told him to return the next day.

for my second voyage. To begin with, it was a pleasant journey. Then one day, we reached a strange desert island. Many of the passengers decided to go ashore, and I sat down on the bank of a river and fell fast asleep. When I awoke, there was not a soul in sight. The ship had sailed, for the captain had forgotten all about me.

However, I decided to climb a tree and survey the island. It was then that I discovered a great white dome.

Full of hope, I marched in the direction of the dome, but as I drew near, I realised it had no doors. The sun had not yet set and the sky was a fiery pink. Suddenly, everything went dark, as though night had fallen. I looked up and saw an enormous bird with outstretched wings, shutting out the sunlight. I remembered then of hearing about a bird so huge it fed its nestlings on elephants. The bird's name was Rukh. Just then I realised that the dome was really one of Rukh's eggs. Indeed, the great bird settled on top of the egg and dropped off to sleep. I unwound my turban and twisted it to make a rope. I tied the end of it round the bird's leg so that it would carry me away with it. At the first light of dawn, the bird woke, spread its immense wings and took flight. So high did it rise into the sky that the earth almost vanished from sight, but it landed on a plateau. I undid the knot. Rukh floated down into the valley below and when he

The following day, after providing the porter and the other guests with a delicious meal, Sinbad the Sailor again began to speak.

"One day, I again had a great desire to travel. I decided to invest some of my money in trading goods and went on board ship at Bassora

returned, it was with a large snake in his beak. Nobody lived on this plateau and, on the other side of the valley lay a mountain far too high for anyone ever to climb.

All I could do was clamber down into the valley. When I got there, I saw the ground was littered with diamonds and full of terrible snakes. I couldn't help shuddering. Luckily, the snakes were not moving about that day, for fear of Rukh, but darkness was about to fall. I found a cave and blocked the entrance with a rock.

In the morning, I left the cave and started to roam the valley searching for a way out. Suddenly I came upon the carcass of an animal. Just then I remembered once hearing the story of a doomed valley, into which diamond hunters would throw a large dead animal. The precious gems stuck to the carcass and the hunters would then wait for a vulture or eagle to appear. The bird of prey would swoop down on the meat and carry it away in its talons to the plateau above. There, the diamond hunters, shouting and yelling, forced the bird to give up its prey. With this tale in mind, I filled my pockets with diamonds then roped myself to the dead animal.

A little later, a huge eagle carried the carcass and me to the plateau. It was just about to tear into the flesh with its beak, when some men appeared, shouting loudly. The eagle flapped away and, though my clothes were bloodstained, I was alive!

I told the diamond hunters about my adventure and gave some diamonds to the man who had thrown the carcass into the valley. They all told me I was under Allah's own protection. I had come out alive

203

from the valley of the snakes; something nobody else had ever done before. Next day, I set off homewards. I bartered some of the diamonds for goods to sell and became richer than ever. When I arrived in Baghdad, my friends and relations welcomed me with delight and, again forgetting all my trials and troubles, I went back to an easy life. And that's the tale of my second voyage.

I'll tell you about the third tomorrow. It's time to eat now," ended Sinbad the Sailor.

Sinbad the bearer of burdens had, like all those present, listened wide-eyed to this story, and again that evening, he found himself gifted another three gold coins. Of course, next day, he hurried back to the sailor's home. He sat at his side till the rich man's friends came, then they sat down to a cheerful feast. When the meal was over, Sinbad the Sailor told the tale of his third voyage.

"Rich as I was, I wanted to become even richer. So I got a passage again at Bassora, on a fine vessel, together with other merchants.

One day, we ran into a fierce storm and the captain began to cry:

'The ship is out of control! The sails are in tatters! Let's hope we can find shelter in the lee of Monkey Mountain. Though the monkeys are dangerous beasts!'

Shortly after this, the ship ran aground on the shore of a strange island and, in next to no time, we were surrounded by a tribe of monkeys. About the height of a child, hairy and smelly, they rushed about as we stood there without moving a muscle, afraid of what they might do. All we could do was stand aside and watch them swarm up the masts and tear the rubber lifeboats with their sharp teeth.

Soon after, a giant wave swept the vessel out to sea, with the horrid creatures still aboard, together with all our cargo. As we wandered over the island, we caught sight of a huge castle-like building. Though very much afraid, we ventured through the gateway. The castle looked deserted, but somebody certainly lived there for, in the middle of the courtyard stood a large bench and a bonfire of logs was ablaze.

We all sank on to the bench and, overcome by fatigue, fell fast asleep. As evening came the ground began to tremble. A terrifying creature was approaching us. It was a real ogre, gigantic with fierce red eyes, long fangs like those of a wild pig, a great mouth and huge ears. The ogre grabbed me and started to prod me with his enormous hands. Luckily I was too skinny for his taste, so he picked out the plumpest of my companions, killed and made a meal of him. After this meal, he stretched out on the bench and slept while we shrank trembling in a corner, unable to sleep a wink. Next morning, the giant went off after locking the door behind him. For us it was a day of terror and the giant, when he returned, picked out another of our little band and made a meal of him too. As soon as he had fallen asleep, we came to a decision:

'We must kill him while he's asleep!' So we put two long sticks into the coals and when they were burning hot, thrust them into the giant's eyes. The ogre leapt to his feet with a scream, knocking us over as he did. Now blinded, he was quite unable to catch us. He fumbled his way to the door and stumbled out, screaming horribly as he went. We ran as fast as we could down to the sea and hastily made a raft out of pieces of driftwood. The raft was barely in the water when we saw the giant coming, with an even more horrible-looking giantess.

They started to hurl great rocks at us, and we were hit more than once. Before we could escape their reach, they had managed to kill all my companions except two. Though by now the raft was scarcely afloat, it carried all three of us to another island. Not knowing where we were, we roamed all day, meeting no-one at all, and fell sound asleep when night fell.

It was not a peaceful night, however. A giant snake crept up and gobbled down one of my friends. Then it curled up and went to sleep. Shaking with terror, my remaining companion and I climbed a tree. Thinking he was sure to be safe there, my friend settled down in the lowest forked branch. This was to save my life. For the snake later finding the poor man an easy victim, ate him up rather than climb to the top of the tree for me. I didn't see how I could ever get away from this place alive. However, I had an idea. Picking up the planks lying round about, I tied one under my feet, another on each side, one along my stomach, another at my back and the last as a roof over my head. This gave me a sort of armour. When, late that night, the snake did its best to devour me, it could not, no matter how hard it tried. My wooden armour withstood the crushing. The reptile squeezed and squeezed till dawn, but as the sun came up, it wearily gave up and slithered away. I untied the planks and set off in search of food. My wanderings took me to the tip of the island, high above the sea. As I sat there, downhearted, staring at the water, I saw a ship sail past, only a few hundred yards from the shore. The crew heard my cries and I was safe at last. I was hoisted aboard, fed and clothed and later I told them my amazing tale, which naturally astonished those who heard it. A fair wind swept us safely into the port of Salahita.

The captain then said to me:

'You're a poor unfortunate stranger here, but I'd like to give you another chance. This ship is carrying a batch of goods belonging to one of the passengers who vanished on a desert island. Nothing has ever been heard of him again. I'm going to sell these articles and take the money back to his family. If you like, you can try selling them. I'll give you a commission on what you manage to sell.'

I thanked the captain for his kindness; I was desperately in need. However, the bosun who was busy listing the cargo, asked a question:

'Captain,' he said, 'what name do I put on these goods?'

'Mark them as Sinbad the Sailor's. That's the name of the man who disappeared.'

'But *I'm* Sinbad the Sailor!' I exclaimed. 'And I didn't disappear at all. I fell asleep on the island and when I awoke, you had all gone. These are my goods. The diamond hunters I met on the mountain, to whom I told my tale, will vouch for all this.'

The crowd of seamen and merchants that had clustered round to listen, began to murmur amongst themselves. Some believed my words, others swore I was a liar. Suddenly, however, on hearing the words 'diamond hunters', one of the merchants came up to me and, after a good stare, exclaimed:

'Do you remember when I told you all about the man roped to the carcass I threw into Diamond Valley? Well, this is him! I know his face. Everything he says is true.' At that, the captain sharply demanded:

'What marks do your goods have on them? Which are they?' I told him and he too realised that I was none other than Sinbad. That's how I got my belongings back and was able to go on trading as though nothing had happened. When I returned home, I saw that I was even richer than before. That's all I have to tell about my third voyage," Sinbad said, "but if you come back tomorrow, I'll describe the fourth one."

Thus saying, he ordered that the bearer of burdens should be given three gold coins. Next morning, Sinbad the Porter hurried back to his rich friend. They enjoyed a meal and waited till all the other guests had appeared. Then Sinbad the Sailor started to tell the story of his fourth adventure.

"As in the past, I began to feel the urge to travel, and I knew I had to go back to sea. I bought a great quantity of goods, said goodbye and went to Bassora to find a ship. To begin with, the voyage was all plain sailing. Till the day a hurricane ripped the sails and broke up the ship. We all ended in the sea, though most of us were able to cling to bits of wreckage and keep afloat.

Then the waters grew calm again and the waves washed us ashore on an island. Our first thought was to look for food and as we did so, we came upon a building. A band of naked men rushed out, without uttering a sound and shut us up in a large pen. They brought us such strange food that I, who did not trust them, refused to eat. But, overcome by hunger, my friends gobbled it down. This was to lead to their ruin, for the more they ate, as though by magic, the hungrier they felt.

In horror, I realised that the naked men were the subjects of an ogre. They caught shipwrecked sailors, fattened them up with special food and then when they were nice and plump, strangled and roasted them. While my friends, already out of their minds, were led to pasture just like farm animals, I began to starve. By the time I was nothing but skin and bone, nobody was paying the slightest attention to me and I took the opportunity to run away.

For seven days and seven nights I walked without stopping. At dawn on the ei hth da , in the distance I could see folk picking peppers. They took pity on me and led me to their king. I told His Majesty every-thing that had happened since the day I left Baghdad, and feeling sorry for me, the king presented me with a silver coin. I decided to stay in that hospitable city. It was easy to make friends with the citizens, and they soon had great respect for me. One day, I noticed that everyone, the rich and the poor, always rode bareback. Surprised at this, I men-tioned it to the king and he asked

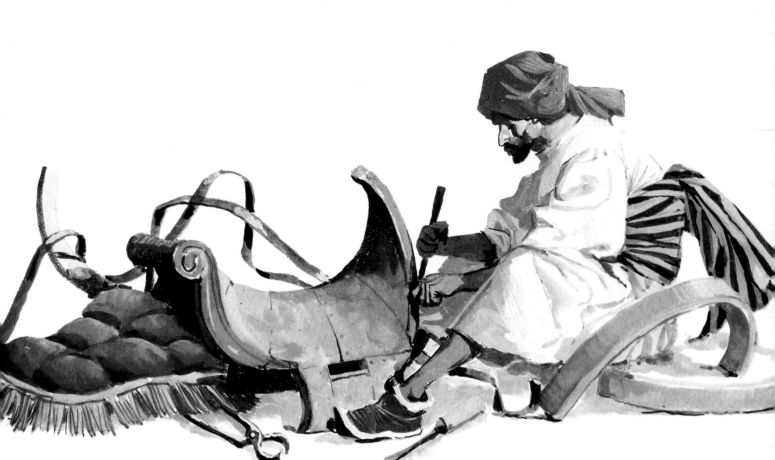

'What is a saddle like?'

'Have I your permission to make one?' I asked him.

'If you wish,' he replied, ordering his servants to provide me with everything I required. A skilled carpenter built the wooden shape, stuffed it with wool and covered it with leather. A blacksmith forged the stirrups. Then I strapped the saddle on a horse's back and persuaded the king to try riding it. He was so delighted that he gave me a generous reward for my work. A few days later, I had a visit from the Prime Minister. He too wanted a saddle, and in the end, so did many other important officials at Court. I set to work at making saddles for them all and quickly became wealthy.

As time went by, my reputation grew, and the king sent for me one day.

'You are now highly respected and well loved by all here. But what you need is a wife. I wish you to marry the young lady I've chosen for you.' And this I did willingly, for she was rich and beautiful. I was perfectly happy with my wife and lived in peace.

'If I ever go home,' I said to myself, 'I'll take her with me.' But a man's fate is always a mystery.

A little time later, I went to visit one of my neighbours. His wife had died and he was desperate.

'My good friend,' I consoled him, 'don't torment yourself like this. You've still a life to live. Maybe you'll get married again and find a

209

wife that is even better than your first one!'

'How do you expect me to remarry,' the man replied, 'when I've only one more day to live!'

'What? But you're perfectly healthy!'

'I know,' he said, 'but I shall be buried along with my wife today. That's our custom.' And as we were speaking, in came the man's friends and relations. The dead woman was gently laid in her coffin and carried to the foot of a hill by the sea shore. There the gravediggers lifted up a great stone, revealing a deep pit. Once the coffin had been lowered into the pit, the widower was obliged to follow it down, taking with him nothing but a jug of water and seven pieces of bread. I cried, 'That's a fate worse than death.' I hurried straight to the king. 'How can anyone be so cruel as to bury the living with the dead?' I asked him.

'It isn't cruel,' he replied. 'This custom has been followed since the dawn of time.'

'Do strangers suffer the same fate?' I asked him.

'Yes. It touches all who live in this land and have married here.'

I was aghast. This meant that *my* life would be linked to my wife's, and if she were to die, I would be buried with her. By sheer ill luck, my wife did fall ill some time after

and died only a few days later. Her relatives arrived, dressed her, adorning her with all her jewellery, then laid her in her coffin. They firmly gripped me and though I struggled and protested, I was lowered into the pit. The stone clanged back into place over my head. Wild with terror, I fainted. When I came to my senses I could see, with the aid of a feeble light filtering from a tiny crack, that I was in a vast cavern. All around, amongst broken coffins, lay skeletons covered with jewels. Horror gave way to madness. I started to gather up the precious stones, without thinking that I would never be able to take them out, for this place was to be my own tomb. Overcome by desperation, I screamed, wept and swore, before dropping exhausted by the wall of the cavern.

The days passed. I had carefully rationed my bread and water to make it last. I soon lost all notion of time and had no idea how long I had been down this pit. Yet a small ray of hope shone within me. I had survived so many other adventures and trials that it seemed impossible that I should die now. One day, the noise of rolling stones wakened me from sleep. I leapt to my feet and rushed towards the spot the sound seemed to come from. There I saw a huge badger which, alarmed at my sudden arrival, fled along a tunnel. I followed it and after crawling for what seemed an eternity, caught sight of light: it was the hole in the rock through which the badger had entered.

In the open air again, I found

myself halfway up the hillside. Fresh air at last! I felt as though I had been given a new lease of life. However, I went back along the tunnel to the cavern and stripped the dead of the jewels they would never need again.

On the shore I managed to catch some lobsters and other molluscs. The days went by, and at last I saw a ship. I rushed to the top of the hill and waved a white cloth. Luckily someone saw it and a lifeboat was

lowered into the water. I was soon aboard, safe and sound. The ship continued on its way. It was an uneventful voyage, and some days later, I returned to Baghdad and my family and friends. And that," said Sinbad, "is what happened to me on my fourth sea voyage."

With that, the sailor fell silent and his guests remarked in tones of wonder about their host's adventures. It was late when the porter rose to his feet to leave, and again he found three gold coins slipped into his hand.

At the first light of dawn next day, Sinbad the Porter went to the house of Sinbad the Sailor, who began to tell another tale.

"I was as good as dead more than once during my fourth voyage, but I soon forgot the risks I had run. I began to feel the wanderlust again. This time I bought a ship, signed on a captain and loaded it with cargo. We sailed and traded from one island to another, till one day, we dropped anchor in a bay of a desert island. Far in the distance I could see a white dome. It was a huge egg. That's when I knew I had landed on Rukh's island. Though I warned the merchants not to, they broke the egg and took out the chick. Just as they were about to cook it, the sky grew very dark.

Rukh's wings had blotted out the sun. We all ran back to the ship and I shouted to cast off immediately. When Rukh saw that the egg was broken, off he flew in search of his mate.

In a very short time, the two great birds came back, circled above the ship for a moment or two, then flapped away. We were well out to sea when we spotted the birds, each gripping a boulder in its talons. The captain managed to swerve and avoid Rukh's rock, but the second boulder scored a direct hit on the prow, smashing it to bits. The ship sank like a stone.

As luck would have it, fate floated a spar towards me and clinging to this, I was washed by the tide onto an island beach. I found myself in an immense garden of Eden, thickly planted with fruit trees and full of sparkling streams. After wandering through this garden for a while, I came upon an old man dressed in leaves, beside a spring. Thinking he must be another shipwrecked sailor, I went over to him.

Without saying a word, the old man gestured that he wanted to go into the nearby forest, but was unable to walk. So I hoisted him onto my shoulders. However, when we reached the spot I thought he had pointed to, he refused to get down. What's more, as I tried to shrug him off my back, he squeezed his legs so tightly round my neck, I almost choked. I fell to the ground and the stranger began to kick me with an energy that was amazing in one so old and so small. Then I realised I was at his mercy. Indeed, by dint of kicking, he made me carry him here and there, without a moments rest. The only time I got any rest was when he fell asleep. But these breaks were very short, for the old fellow would not let me be. Dazed by his blows, I was furious at being so ill-rewarded for my kindness in helping him in the first place.

As I was wandering about one day with the old man on my back, I saw some large water melons in a field. Close by was a vineyard, the vines laden with grapes. I decided I could easily make some wine. The old man said he did not mind and let me get on with the job. Several days later, the grapes had fermented and when the old fellow saw me happily tasting the wine, he snatched the gourd from my hands and drained it dry. A little later, he was flat on the ground, helplessly drunk. I kicked him then as hard as I could and ran off.

A few days after this, a storm drove a ship into the bay, where she dropped anchor. I was taken aboard, given fresh clothes and a meal. When the storm had passed, the ship set sail and some weeks later we reached the monkey town. This strange town got its name from the ferocious monkeys that invaded it every evening. Towards sundown, the citizens were obliged to leave the town, take refuge on ships and other craft and stay away from the shore. Anyone remaining in the town would be killed by these fearsome creatures. Here too I had another stroke of bad luck.

Having left the ship and gone to visit the town, I lingered at the market and my ship left without me. I was roaming about feeling very frightened, for it was almost evening, when a man came over to me.

'Come with me,' he said, 'or the

monkeys will get you!' So I went aboard his boat and spent the night out at sea, returning with the rest of the people in the morning. And for the rest of the time I passed on the island, I spent the night on this man's boat. The owner became a friend and he said to me:

'What's your job? What skills do you have?'

'I'm a merchant,' I replied, 'but I can't trade, for I've lost all I had.'

'Take this sack then,' he said 'fill it with stones. Go with these men and do as they do! Maybe you'll manage to make some money.' So I filled the sack with stones and went with the other men to a palm grove on the outskirts of the town, the home of a tribe of monkeys. The men started to throw the stones at the beasts, and from their perches in the treetops, the monkeys threw coconuts. Whether this was in imitation of the men or in self defence, I do not know. But when we had thrown all our stones, we filled the sacks with coconuts. Back in the town, I took my coconut harvest to my friend.

'Sell as many as you need to and store the rest in my warehouse.' I could not thank him enough for his help. Every day I went to the palm grove and came back laden with coconuts. I sold some and stored the rest in the warehouse.

Then one fine day, a ship sailed in. Now was my chance to go home again. I agreed a price with the captain for taking me and my load of coconuts. We set sail immediately, calling at islands and ports, and at all of them I bartered coconuts. On Cinnamon Island I bought cinnamon, on Pepper

Island, I got a large quantity of pepper. Then we landed on an island where the aloe trees grew. The wood of this tree is the best in the world and I bought a large number of planks. Later, we came to the Pearl Sea. I called the fishermen and promised them many coconuts if they would fish pearls for me. This they did, and they brought me lots of big pearls.

'You have a great fortune there, Sir,' the fishermen exclaimed. Never before had they found so many big pearls all at the one time. With the blessing of Allah, we had an easy trip to Bassora, where I stopped for some time before going

on to Baghdad. There I found my home, family and all my friends again. I gave generously, especially to widows and orphans, as I always did. When all was said and done, I had succeeded in gaining nearly four times the amount I had lost. That helped me to quickly forget all my misadventures and I soon dropped back into a carefree, happy-go-lucky life.

"Go now!" said Sinbad the Sailor, "but return tomorrow, and I'll tell you what happened during my sixth voyage."

Sinbad the Porter received his usual three gold coins and went off home. Next morning, he returned, and was greeted with Sinbad the Sailor's usual kindliness. When the other guests arrived, there was a cheerful feast and all those present praised the sailor's generosity. After the meal, Sinbad began to tell his tale.

"Well, friends, I was so delighted to be back that my life was a round of parties and festivities. Once more I forgot all my past suffering, fears and brushes with death. One day, certain merchants who had just returned from a long cruise, came to see me, and I was seized with the longing to set out on my travels. So I bought new goods and took a passage on a large ship. It was a peaceful voyage till the day the captain announced in frightened tones:

'The wind has blown us into unknown waters. Anything can happen now, for I have no idea if there are reefs and rocks. I have no charts that show these seas. All we can do is pray to Allah!' Still greatly alarmed, he set the sails to quickly leave behind the uncharted waters. But the wind suddenly veered, so violently that the rudder split apart, leaving us at the mercy of the waves, a short distance from an island surrounded by terrifying rocks.

'There's no hope for us at all!'

cried the captain. And a second later, the ship crashed onto the rocks, smashing into a thousand splinters. With one or two others, I managed to cling to a rock. We came later to a wide beach, encircled by a steep mountain. Wreckage from many a shipwreck lay scattered on the shore. Beside the beach, a river flowed for a short distance before disappearing into an opening in the rock. We quickly discovered that things of value were to be found amongst the wrecks and we picked up rubies, pearls, emeralds and diamonds.

Our great fear, however, was of

dying of hunger for, though there were a few trees, not one bore any signs of fruit or even a berry to eat. And so, within a few days, everyone had died but myself, and I knew that I could not last long. I decided to dig my own grave.

'If I should feel too weak,' I told myself, 'I shall lay myself down in my coffin and wait for death. Then the wind will blow sand over me and I too will have a proper burial.' I dug the hole, then sat down to await the end, on the bank of the river, cursing my craze for travel. As I gazed at the running water, I suddenly realised that it must be flowing somewhere, perhaps even to a place where people were living. I had to make a raft. With that thought, I set to work using driftwood from the beach. Now, in order to float through the entrance to the rock, the raft would have to be short and narrow, so I made it the same length as my own height and found two short sticks as oars. I loaded all the gems I had found and my remaining items of food. Then I shoved it into the water and lay down on it.

The current swept me under the shadow of the rock and into darkness. The raft floated along, brushing the walls of the underground passageway, ready to capsize from one minute to the next. Then the tunnel widened and the raft glided so smoothly and so gently that I fell asleep.

When I awoke, I was back in the open air, lying on the grassy river bank and surrounded by men. Their friendly looks quickly calmed my fears.

'Welcome, brother,' said one of the men as I opened my eyes. 'Where have you come from? Who

are you?' I almost shouted at him:
' In the name of all-holy Allah!
Give me a bite of food. Then I'll
answer all your questions.' At once
the kindly people brought me food
and drink, and as I gobbled it hun-
grily, I told them my tale.

'We must take you to our king,'
said the men. 'This is an extraordinary story. He'll be interested to hear
it.' A few hours later, we were in the
city. My new friends had brought
the raft too, with its load. The king
gave me a splendid welcome,
listened to my tale and said how
glad he was I had scraped through.
Being curious to hear about life in

my own land, he asked me to stay as
his guest.

'I've learned a lot from you,' he
told me. 'The Caliph of Baghdad
seems to be a wise ruler. I wish to
send him a gift as a token of friendship and respect. I'd like you to take
it to him when you return to your
own city.'

Not long after, a group of merchants engaged a ship to sail to
Bassora. This was my chance. I
went to the king and told him I
wanted to leave. And with great
courtesy, since I was to take his gift
to the Caliph of Baghdad, he paid
all my travelling expenses.

The moment I reached Baghdad, I called on the Caliph with the gift. He was amazed and wondered why an unknown king should be so generous. So I told him what had happened. I spent almost a whole week at the Caliph's court, for the ruler never tired of hearing me repeat my story. At long last, I was free to return home, and I carefully laid my treasure in my strong boxes. And this is the adventure of the sixth voyage," ended Sinbad the Sailor. The porter was handed his three gold coins and off he went. Back he came at sunrise next day, and again Sinbad the Sailor began to recount.

"As before, I craved to travel after a while. For a long time, we had fair winds. Then one day, a storm blew up, bringing driving rain, like nothing we had ever seen before.

But this was not all, for a little later, the captain began to tear his hair in desperation as he cried:

'Pray Allah if we're to be saved! This is the sea of the doomed, from which there is no return.' Then he took a fistful of earth from a box, dampened it with seawater, sniffed it and went on to say:

'Men, this is a strange part of the world we're in, with evil forces. We've no hope of escape. We are close to the land where King Solomon is buried, and the home of huge deadly snakes. Ships here are swallowed by monster fish!' Hardly had the captain said these words than there was a terrible roar, like the sound of a thousand tempests. In a flash a giant fish rose from the deep and swam towards us. We had barely set eyes on this, when a

second and then another even more gigantic fish broke the surface of the sea. All three splashed round and round us, then the biggest hurled itself at our ship, its jaws gaping wide to swallow us. At that very instant, a great wave heaved the ship into the air and threw it against the rocks. Everyone on board was knocked into the sea. Gasping for breath, I managed to grab a plank. Then I found I was alone, for all the others had drowned.

'If I get out of here alive,' I cried, 'I swear to Allah that I'll never again leave Baghdad.' For two days and nights I floated in the sea, but on the third day, my feet located dry land. I was on an island, and as I explored it, I came to a river that reminded me of my previous voyage. Perhaps this river too would carry me to safety.

Again I needed a raft, and set about finding suitable bits of wood. Luckily, I laid hands on some precious sandalwood, which is light and floats well. The raft was soon ready and I set off down the river. For two days, everything went smoothly, but on the third day, the current dragged me in the direction of a cave. Terror-stricken, I tried in vain to pole the raft to the bank, but the river carried me into the heart of

the mountain. This time the tunnel was not very long, but a series of waterfalls boomed and echoed like thunder and I was battered and beaten by the rushing waters. At long last, after running the risk of being smashed to pieces against the rocks, the river again flowed calmly and carried me along till I came to a city.

By that time I was half dead from hunger and terror. An old man with a white beard took me home and gave me shelter. Some days later, he said to me.

'Come with me, my son, to the market and sell your goods.' I could not understand what he meant. What goods? But I said nothing. Then I discovered that the sandalwood, of which the raft was

made, was valuable in that country. And so, I again became rich. The old man grew so fond of me he wanted me to marry his only daughter. I had no choice but to agree. In any case, his daughter was kind and beautiful, as well as rich. Time passed and the old man died. I inherited his worldly goods and also his position as chief of the merchants.

But I quickly made an amazing discovery about some of the inhabitants of the city: on the first day of each month, certain men grew wings, rose into the air and flew far out of sight. The next day, they went back to everyday life.

The first day of the next month, I approached one of the winged men and jumped on his back. Off we flew, higher and higher into the sky, almost touching the vaults of heaven, and I thought I heard the angels sing. Overcome by emotion, I couldn't help calling out:

'Praise and Glory be to Allah!' I had hardly said the last word when a giant tongue of fire leapt from the sky, just missing us by inches. We dived down to the peak of a high mountain and the winged man yelled at me in rage:

'You spoiled everything, praising Allah while we were flying!'

'I never dreamt that it would do any

harm,' I replied. 'I'm very sorry. Please take me back to the city.' The man agreed, on condition that I made no mention of Allah while on his back. He took me straight home where my wife, worried at my absence, was delighted to see me. When I told her what had happened, she said:

'You were naive. You mustn't go near these folk. They're brothers to the Devil and hate the name of Allah.'

'What about your father?' I asked.

'My father never had anything to do with them, and never did anything wrong. He wanted me to marry you so there would be no danger of my becoming the wife of a winged man. Why don't you sell everything and let's go together to Baghdad?' I took her advice and some months later, we came home. Here I saw friends and relatives who had given up all hope of ever setting eyes on me again, and they gave us a great homecoming.

Everyone was astonished to hear my story, but all were overjoyed when I swore that I had been on my last voyage. And this was also my last adventure," concluded the host.

"Please excuse me for my complaints when I didn't know you and had no idea how much you had gone through to become rich," said Sinbad the Porter. Sinbad the Sailor hugged him and asked him to remain in his house as a guest. And from that day on, Sinbad the Sailor and Sinbad the Porter lived together as brothers.

PRINCE OMAR AND PRINCESS SHEHERAZADE

Once upon a time, on the island of Kaledan, lived a king who was famous all over the East, well-loved by his subjects and respected even by his enemies. In spite of having a good and beautiful wife, his life was not always happy. After years of marriage, they had no children and were afraid they would never know the joy of a family.

However, at long last, one splendid spring morning, a handsome baby boy was born and his delighted parents called him Omar. In the language of Kaledan, this means "shining light". The years went by and Omar grew into a fine-looking youth, brave, intelligent and kind-hearted.

On his eighteenth birthday, the king sent for his son.

"Omar, now that you've come of age, you must find a wife. Choose one of the many princesses you've met and whose only dream is of marrying you."

"Father," said Omar respectfully, "I've no intention of getting married. I'm still young and I'd rather wait till the time is ripe. I want to think about it for at least another year." The king agreed and Omar spent the year studying with the wisest and cleverest teachers in the kingdom. And though he got to know a number of girls, he did not fall in love. When twelve months had passed, the young prince was

again summoned to his father.

"Well, son," said the king anxiously, "when am I to announce your engagement?"

"Alas, father, I still haven't met the right girl," was Omar's reply. The king lost his temper.

"Omar! You must stop wasting time. You're a grown man now and I want to see your heirs. Think of the future and make up your mind without delay."

"I'm sorry, father, I can't do that just yet. I'm not in love and so I can't get married." The king, who could not bear to be crossed in such an important matter, went into a rage. He shouted for the guards and ordered them to shut the prince in an old castle in the forest.

In the meanwhile, lovely sweet-natured Princess Sheherazade was

a maiden whose home was in China. When she became sixteen years old, her father insisted she marry one of the princes that flocked to court her. But Sheherazade was waiting to meet a true love. And since nothing the king, her father, did served to change her mind, he locked the princess up in one of the palaces.

"I'd rather be a prisoner," said the princess, "than have a husband I didn't love."

Meantime, Omar spent lonely sad days in the castle where he was held prisoner. However, two in-visible genies, Abhu and Dhabi were amusing themselves, un-known to the prince, by secretly watching his movements. One day Abhu said to his friend:

"Omar is the most handsome person in the whole world."

"Not so!" exclaimed Dhabi. "The most beautiful person in the world is Sheherazade, the King of China's daughter." The genies started to argue, then decided to ask Lilibeth, the daughter of the genie king to judge the matter. Lilibeth's advice was this:

"Go to China, cast a sleeping

spell over the princess and bring her to Omar's castle. When you see them together, then you'll soon see which is the most beautiful." That very night Abhu and Dhabi flew all the way to China. The two genies sent the princess to sleep and carried her to Omar's castle.

"They're so lovely, they seem made for each other," remarked the genies, gazing at the two young people together. "If only they could get to know each other . . ." And in the hope that they might, the genies hid behind a curtain and waited . . .

Not long afterwards, Sheherazade opened her eyes and, when she saw Omar at her side, her heart began to thump. This was the man she would like to marry. So she took off one of her rings and slipped it on to his finger as a token of love. Then she went back to sleep. On wakening a little later, Omar set eyes on Sheherazade and was overwhelmed by her beauty.

"If this girl is as kind as she's beautiful, she would make a wonderful wife," said Omar to himself as he gazed at her in amazement. Then he took off a ruby ring and slipped it onto the princess's finger. Drowsy again, he fell asleep. Abhu and Dhabi crept out from behind the curtain, wide-eyed.

"They've fallen in love," said Dhabi. "What are we to do now?" "Take Sheherazde home again. But if they have really fallen in love, they'll move heaven and earth to meet again."

And so, when Omar awoke, Sheherazade had vanished. Confused and upset, the prince asked his guards and servants if they had seen her. When the king heard the story, he told Omar:
"My lad, you are losing your head over a girl you dreamed about!"
"No, she wasn't a dream," the

prince insisted. "This is the ring she left me!" Omar was lovesick. The king called doctors and wise men, but there was nothing they could do, for Omar was losing his will to live.

And far away, Sheherazade was pining in sorrow. The king was certain his daughter must have dreamt it all. How otherwise could she have met the mysterious young man? The only person who believed the princess was Marzuan, a childhood friend, and he offered to search for the missing youth. Sheherazade handed him Omar's

ruby ring. Marzuan set out that same day but, though he travelled far and wide, no-one could give him a clue as to the young man's identity.

In the meantime, Abhu and Dhabi secretly followed in his tracks. One day, a merchant told Marzuan that, on the island of Kaledan, there was a lovesick prince. Feeling that this might be the very person he was seeking, Marzuan took a passage on a ship bound for Kaledan. After days of sailing, a terrible storm broke, driving the ship onto a reef, where it sank. Clinging to a floating spar, Marzuan held on till the storm died away, then headed for the shore. The beach was deserted, but in the distance he could see the turrets of a castle. Then, as he was getting his strength back, he saw a horseman approach.

"Where am I?" Marzuan asked the stranger.

"On the island of Kaledan," replied the horseman. "Who are you?" Marzuan jumped to his feet.

"I'm a doctor, and famous in my own land. I hear that a prince here is seriously ill, and I'd like to try and cure him."

"Yes," replied the horseman, "Prince Omar is indeed seriously ill, but it seems his illness is fatal." Disturbed by his words, Marzuan said:

"Take me to him straight away." When admitted to Omar's presence, without saying a word, Marzuan showed him the ruby ring. Omar uttered a shriek and leapt to his feet. The onlookers stared in surprise.

"This is the ring I gave to the girl I want to marry!" the prince exclaimed joyfully.

"That young lady is Sheherazade.

231

She lives in far off China and is dying to see you again," Marzuan told him instantly. Omar was delighted. In finding the girl of his dreams, he would be truly happy.

He presented Marzuan with a jewelled sword and a splendid horse, as fast as the wind, as a token of thanks. Then he told him to take him as quickly as could be to the beautiful princess. Overcoming all the difficulties that it had to face during the long journey, the cheer-

ful procession led by Omar and Marzuan, many days later, reached distant China. When they reached Sheherazade's city, Omar announced his arrival by sending a messenger with a letter for the princess and a diamond ring.

At long last, the couple had met again. They exchanged their first, affectionate words and found they really were meant for each other. Sure of their feelings and anxious to start a new life together, Omar and

Sheherazade quickly asked the king's permission to get married as soon as possible.

The invisible genies, Abhu and Dhabi too, were at the wedding, a few days later.

"Sheherazade really *is* lovely!" Dhabi exclaimed.

"Yes, but Omar . . ." said Abhu.

"Are you looking for an argument again?" demanded Dhabi. Just then, Lilibeth, the genie king's daughter appeared.

"We still haven't decided which is the better-looking," said Abhu and Dhabi.

"Well, I'd say they are the best-looking couple in the world," said Lilibeth. "And I'm certain their children will be even more handsome."

And so the argument finally

ended to everybody's satisfaction, and the two genies hugged each other contentedly.

THE FLYING TRUNK

Once upon a time, many years ago in Copenhagen, in Denmark, a wealthy merchant had a son called Erik. Erik was a good-looking lad, intelligent too, but very lazy. Instead of studying or doing some work, he liked to spend his days roaming about, amusing himself with his friends and squandering his father's money on unnecessary luxuries. When the merchant died, he left all his money to Erik, who frittered it away in a matter of months.

The only thing left was an empty magic trunk. The minute anyone stepped inside, it rose into the air. One day, Erik, who had no intention of working for a living, decided to face the unknown and seek his fortune. So he stepped into the trunk and, for days on end, flew across the seas and over woodlands and deserts. At last, he found himself above a city in the East and ordered the trunk to land on the terrace of a wonderful palace. Erik stepped out of the trunk and there in front of him stood a girl, staring at him in amazement.

"I'm Tamara, the Sultan's daughter," she said. "Who are you?" Quick to turn the situation to his own advantage, Erik replied:

"I'm the god of your people, come to ask your hand in marriage." Fascinated by the handsome stranger and certain that he really was a god, she happily said 'yes' and called her family. The Sultan welcomed the youth with great honours and immediately started to make arrangements for the wedding.

The day before the ceremony, Erik stuffed the trunk full of jewels, golden candle sticks and fine damasks and flew away from the palace towards Copenhagen. However, weighed down by its valuable load, the trunk fell into the sea off the Danish coast. Erik managed to swim ashore and return to Copenhagen, where he sang sad songs at street corners for a living. In the East, on the terrace of a magnificent palace, a young girl sadly glanced at the sky from time to time, hoping that the god who had suddenly disappeared, would come back again.

THE LITTLE PEAR GIRL

Once upon a time, a peasant worked hard to make a living from his land. Every year his pear tree produced four basketfuls of fruit, which had to be given to the king, a greedy ruler who grew rich at the expense of the poor.

One year, part of the pear harvest went bad and the peasant was able to pick only three and a half baskets of fruit. The poor man was beside himself with fear, for the king refused to take less than four basketfuls, and the peasant would be cruelly punished.

All he could do was put his youngest daughter into one of the baskets and cover her with a layer of pears, so that the basket looked full. The king's servants took away the four baskets without ever noticing the trick, and the little girl found herself all alone in the pantry, under the pears.

One day, the cook went into the pantry and discovered her. Nobody could understand where on earth she had come from, and not knowing what to do with her, it was decided she should become a maid in the castle. Folk called her Violetta, for her eyes reminded them of the colour of violets.

Violetta was a pretty girl, sweet

and generous. One day, as she was watering the flowers in the royal gardens, she met the king's son, a youth of her own age, and the two became friends. The other maids, jealous of Violetta's beauty and of the affection many people in the castle felt for the girl, did everything they could to get her into trouble, by spreading nasty rumours about her. One day, the king sent for her and said severely:

"I'm told you boast of being able to steal the witches' treasure trove. Is that true?" Violetta said 'no,' but the king refused to believe her and drove her out of his kingdom.

"You may return only when you have laid hands on the treasure," he said. All Violetta's fondest friends, including the prince, were sorry to hear of the king's decision, but could do nothing to stop her going. The girl wandered through the forest and, when she came to a pear tree, she climbed into its branches and fell asleep. She was wakened at dawn by an old woman calling her:

"What are you doing up there, all by yourself?" Violetta told the old woman her tale. She offered to help the little girl, gave her some round loaves, a broom, a little oil and some good advice, and the girl again set off. She reached a clearing with a large wood stove and saw three women tearing their hair, using it to sweep the ashes from the stove. Violetta offered them the broom and the women pointed out the way to the witches' palace.

Suddenly, two hungry mastiffs

blocked her path. Violetta threw them the loaves, the dogs ate them and let her pass. Then she came to the bank of a river in flood, but remembering the old woman's advice, she sang:

Clear sparkling river

Let me cross over,

and the minute her song wafted into the air, the water stopped flowing. Violetta thus crossed the river and at last reached the witches' palace. The door was unlocked, but Violetta could not push it open for the hinges were rusted. So she rubbed on a little oil and the door swung open. The little girl walked through the empty halls till she came to a splendid room in which lay a mag-

nificent coffer full of jewels. Holding the coffer under her arm, Violetta made for the door, but the coffer, being enchanted, cried out:

"Door! Don't let her out!" However, the door *did* open, for Violetta had oiled the hinges. Down at the river, the coffer cried out. This time it said:

"Water, drown her!" But the river did not stop the little girl from crossing; the two mastiffs did not attack and the three strange women did not burn her in their stove. For each, in its own way, repaid the girl's courtesy. Back at the king's palace again, the prince ran happily to meet Violetta, telling her:

"When my father asks you what

you want as a reward, ask him for the basket of pears in the pantry!" And this Violetta did. Pleased at paying such a modest price, the king instantly ordered the humble basket to be brought. But nobody ever imagined for a minute that underneath the pears lay the prince. The young man came out of his hiding place, swore he was in love with Violetta and that he wanted to marry her.

In this way, the king was forced to give his consent. Violetta brought her family to court and they all began a new and happy life.

THE SNOW QUEEN

There is a legend that, once upon a time, a beautiful fairy, the Snow Queen, lived on the highest, most solitary peaks of the Alps. The mountain folk and shepherds climbed to the summits to admire her, and everyone fell head over heels in love with her.

Every man would have given anything, including his life, to marry her. Indeed, their lives are just what they did give: for Fate had decided that no mortal would every marry the Snow Queen. But in spite of that, many brave souls did their best to approach her, hoping always to persuade her.

Each suitor was allowed to enter the great ice palace with the crystal roof, where the Queen's throne stood. But the second he declared his love and asked for her hand, thousands of goblins appeared to grasp him and push him over the rocks, down into bottomless abysses.

Without the slightest emotion, the Queen would watch the scene, her heart of ice unable to feel anything at all. The legend of the crystal palace and the beautiful heartless Queen spread as far as the most distant alpine valley, the home of a fearless chamois hunter. Fascinated by the tale, he decided to set out and try his luck. Leaving his valley, he journeyed for days on

end, climbing the snowclad mountain faces, scaling icebound peaks and defying the bitterly cold wind that swept through the alpine gullies.

More than once he felt all was lost, but the thought of the lovely Snow Queen gave him new strength and kept him moving onwards. At last, after many days climbing, he saw glinting in the sunshine before him, the tall transparent spires of the ice palace.

Summoning all his courage, the young man entered the Throne Room. But he was so struck by the Snow Queen's beauty that he could not utter a word. Shy and timid, he did not dare speak. So he knelt in admiration before the Queen for hours on end, without opening his mouth. The Queen looked at him silently, thinking all the while that, provided he did not ask her hand in marriage, there was no need to call the goblins.

Then, to her great surprise, she discovered that his behaviour touched her heart. She realised she was becoming quite fond of this hunter, much younger and more handsome than her other suitors. Time passed and the Snow Queen dared not admit, not even to herself, that she would actually like to *marry* the young man.

In the meantime, the goblins kept watch over their mistress; first they were astonished, then they became more and more upset. For they rightly feared that their Queen might be on the point of breaking the Law and bringing down on the heads of all the Mountain People the fury of Fate.

Seeing that the Queen was slow to give the order to get rid of her suitor, the goblins decided to take matters into their own hands. One night, as dusk fell, they slipped out of the cracks in the rock and clustered round the young chamois hunter. Then they hurled him into the abyss. The Snow Queen watched the whole scene from the window, but there was nothing she could do to stop them. However, her icy heart melted, and the beautiful cruel fairy suddenly became a woman.

A tear dropped from her eye, the first she had ever shed. And the Snow Queen's tear fell on to a stone where it turned into a little silvery star.

This was the first edelweiss . . . the flower that grows only on the highest, most inaccessible peaks in the Alps, on the edge of the abyss and precipice . . .

INDEX

The Adventures of Aladdin	101
Ali Baba and the Forty Thieves	112
Bluebeard	44
The Book of Spells	34
Cinderella	5
Dopey Dennis	182
The Elves and the Shoemaker	62
The Emperor's New Clothes	79
The Empress Jowka	26
The Flying Trunk	234
The Game of Chess	38
Jack and the Beanstalk	70
The Little Pear Girl	236
The Parrot Shah	124
The Peasant, the Snake and the Fox	164
Prince Omar and Princess Sheherazade	224
Puss in Boots	149

The Red Dragon 180

Sasha, Mansor and the Storks 140

Sayed's Adventures 16

The Seven Crows 92

The Seven Old Samurai 172

The Shrewd Farmer's Story 66

Sinbad the Sailor 197

Six Able Men 84

The Sleeping Princess 190

The Snow Maiden 14

The Snow Queen 240

The Tail of the Bear 64

Til Ulenspighel 158

The Tin Soldier 53

The Unlucky Warrior 176

The Weeping Princess 134

The Witch in the Tower 170

OTHER TALES IN THIS SERIES
VOL. I

SNOW WHITE AND THE SEVEN DWARFS
HANSEL AND GRETEL
LITTLE RED RIDING HOOD
THE THREE LITTLE PIGS
GOLDILOCKS AND THE THREE BEARS
PINOCCHIO
THE HARE AND THE TORTOISE
THE MUSICIANS OF BREMEN
THE ADVENTURES OF TOM THUMB
BEAUTY AND THE BEAST
THE PIED PIPER OF HAMELIN
THE LITTLE GOLD FISH

and many, many more...